A few minutes ago she'd been angry and scared. Now she was more turned on than she'd ever been in her life.

What Paige was feeling must have shown clearly on her face, because after a second Max's expression changed. For one heartbeat he stopped rubbing her hand and just looked at her. Just looked. She could feel awareness surround them, engulf them. He knew what she was feeling, and as she watched, she saw answering desire in his gaze.

"Danger does this sometimes," he said, his voice soft and deep. "It doesn't mean anything, Paige. You're upset. That's what's causing this reaction."

"If that's true, then why are you feeling it, too?" she asked.

He caressed her hand one last, lingering time and then slowly released her. With a small smile, he said, "'Cause I'm a guy. We're all animals, haven't you heard?"

She'd heard. But this was one animal she wanted.

Dear Reader,

Okay, here's a confession—I love honorable heroes. I know, all heroes should be honorable, right? But the type I love are those who have to make tough choices, the ones who put the well-being of others before their own happiness. A man like my hero, Max Walker.

Max is an honorable guy, so naturally, he hates lying to Paige. But what choice does he have? If he tells her who he really is, she might end up getting hurt. So even though he knows she'll probably hate him because of his lies, he does the right thing. He chooses Paige's safety over his own happiness. Now, that's honorable.

And I love it. I really enjoyed making life difficult for poor Max, but he never disappointed me. Whenever I gave him a tough choice, he did the right thing. Yep, the man's a hero through and through.

No wonder Paige can't resist him. Who could?

I hope you enjoy *Every Step You Take….* And here's to the heroes we love. They make life fun.

All the best,

Liz Jarrett

Books by Liz Jarrett

HARLEQUIN TEMPTATION
827—TEMPTING TESS

Liz
Jarrett

EVERY STEP YOU TAKE...

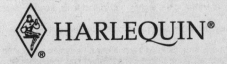

HARLEQUIN®

TORONTO • NEW YORK • LONDON
AMSTERDAM • PARIS • SYDNEY • HAMBURG
STOCKHOLM • ATHENS • TOKYO • MILAN • MADRID
PRAGUE • WARSAW • BUDAPEST • AUCKLAND

To Kathryn Lye,
A wonderful editor and a wonderful person.
Thanks for everything.

ISBN 0-373-69184-X

EVERY STEP YOU TAKE...

Copyright © 2004 by Mary E. Lounsbury.

1

SHE WAS GOING TO MAKE one good-looking corpse, Max Walker decided as he watched Alyssa Paige Delacourte wait tables at the Sunset Café. And there was no doubt about it, if someone was truly after Ms. Delacourte, she was dead meat.

For starters, no one would ever mistake her for a down-and-out waitress. Even in typical Key West barely-there clothing of red shorts and a T-shirt that proclaimed the Sunset Café had the best food in town, the woman's attitude screamed class and money.

Sure, she'd dyed her brown hair a pale blond and went by Paige Harris, her middle name paired with her mother's maiden name, but even a dirtbag like Brad Collier would find her sooner or later.

It had taken Max longer to get his car washed than to find Paige. No wonder her family was worried. They should be. The lady had no idea how to hide.

Deciding to get a little closer, Max headed across the street and found a chair on the restaurant's patio. After working out of Chicago for the past three years, he'd forgotten how hot a place like Key West could get.

But the breeze was cool, the women were gorgeous,

and his bankroll was practically unlimited. All he had to do was to keep sweet Paige from harm.

Piece of cake.

Leaning back in his chair at the small round table, he pulled off his sunglasses and watched Paige first notice him. This close, he couldn't help admiring the view. Paige was one sexy lady. Being blond suited her, but if she wanted to keep a low profile, becoming a blond babe wasn't the way to go. Every guy in the place was watching her.

After a noticeable hesitation, Paige approached him, her walk as sexy as the rest of her. He slowly grinned as she reached his table.

If nothing else, he was going to enjoy guarding this client. Since his last assignment had been a sixty-eight-year-old CEO, watching Paige was definitely a treat.

"May I help you?" She met his gaze straight on. He liked that. She might not be good at hiding, but she wasn't timid.

"Yeah, a beer. Whatever you've got on tap."

She nodded. "Sure. Want anything else?"

Talk about a loaded question. Even though he was on the job, several possibilities ran through his hormone-charged brain.

But he resisted making a comment. No sense scaring her off when he'd just met her. "Naw, just the beer." He blew out a loud breath. "Man, it's hot here."

She nodded. "Guess that comes with the territory. We are as far south as you can get in the continental U.S."

"Seems like a nice place to live." He drummed one hand on the table. "Small, but nice."

"It is." She took a step away. "I'll go get your beer."

He could tell he was spooking her with all the chit-chat. She didn't trust him. Her instincts told her to run.

But since he needed her to trust him, he did his best to distract her. "Hey, know any good places to live around here?" With a self-effacing smile, he added, "Gotta be someplace cheap, though. I just got out of the Navy and don't have a lot in the way of resources."

She narrowed her green eyes as she studied him. He continued to give her his best I-wouldn't-hurt-a-fly smile and waited for her response.

Be a smart lady and don't tell me jack.

For a couple of seconds, she didn't say a word. Just looked at him. He watched with fascination as a small bead of sweat rolled down her neck and slipped under the edge of her T-shirt. She shifted her weight, which only further reminded him of her skimpy shorts and the lush, impressive curves under that T-shirt.

"Any ideas?" he prompted when she still didn't say a word.

She shrugged. "There are lots of places in town."

With a chuckle, he said, "Thanks. That narrows it down."

A light flush colored her cheeks. A lady like Paige wouldn't be used to being rude. But she was being smart. He liked that.

After a couple of seconds, she said, "I don't know you, so I can't say what you'd like. Key West is small, but if you look, you can find some nice places. Beyond that, there's not much I can do to help you."

Deciding to throw her another curve, he said, "Plus you don't *want* to help me because you think I'm hitting on you, so you don't want to tell me squat." He smiled again. "Can't say I blame you. You're cute. Guess lots of guys hit on you."

She blinked. His honesty had obviously caught her off guard.

"I don't think you're hitting on me," she said softly.

"Then you're giving me too much credit."

For the first time since he'd gotten there, she almost smiled. Came close, anyway. One corner of her full lips lifted slightly. Man, she was beautiful. Off-limits, of course. But beautiful.

"I really don't know any places for rent," she said, that pale flush once more coloring her face.

He held her gaze, his grin still firmly tacked in place. He wanted her to think he was just some guy who was looking for a place to stay and enjoyed flirting with pretty ladies. He could feel her sizing him up. She was trying to be smart. Trying to do the right thing.

But an accountant from one of Chicago's oldest families didn't know a thing about running and hiding. And manners were in her upbringing, so he watched in fascination as she struggled to balance her need to be polite with her need to be safe.

"I'll go get your beer," she said finally, her gaze still filled with caution as she reluctantly added, "But good luck finding a place."

She took two steps toward the bar and stopped. She glanced at him, then turned back and headed over to his table. Tearing a sheet of paper off her pad, she drew something and handed it to him.

"There are good apartments a couple of miles from here." She nodded toward the map in his hand. "Maybe you'll find something there."

He glanced at the map, tipping his head to try to understand it. She was sending him on a wild-goose chase. He was sure of it.

"I know my directions stink, but follow Truman until it turns into Roosevelt." She broke eye contact. "Then keep heading north."

Max scratched his jaw and studied her drawing. She was heading him away from her, sending him off. Stuffing the drawing in his pocket, he said, "Thanks."

"No problem." Her green eyes still studied him closely. He could feel her uncertainty. Feel her apprehension. Without saying another word, she turned and headed inside the bar.

He watched her walk away. Paige had a natural sway to her walk that made his libido howl. The lady was classy and sexy as hell. He'd figured on the classy part considering her background. But the sexy part was a big surprise. In the pictures her father had given him, Paige had looked nice. Not sexy. Not hot.

Just nice.

Not a major babe.

Maybe he should have taken some time off between watching Fred Hoffman, the CEO, and signing up for this assignment. Maybe then he wouldn't be affected quite so strongly by Paige.

He glanced at the lady in question and realized he was kidding himself. He could've made love to an entire squad of cheerleaders last night, and he'd still find Paige desirable.

Plus, if he'd taken time off before accepting this assignment, he would have missed the chance to protect Paige. His partner and brother, Travis, would have taken the assignment. Talk about putting a kid in a candy store. Trav wasn't good at resisting temptation, and there was no doubt at all that Paige Harris was a major temptation.

No, it was a good thing he'd been in the office when Paige's father had stopped by. If Brad Collier really was hunting her, then Paige needed serious help on her side.

She needed him. He took his job seriously. This was exactly why he'd stopped being a cop and become a private investigator. He hated when the bad guy won. That feeling had eaten at his gut until he'd had no choice but to quit the force and opened Walker Investigations over five years ago. Trav had joined him two years ago, and they'd never looked back.

In all that time, they'd never lost a client. Never. They'd even protected the ones who'd had some serious trash on their tail. Brad Collier was small potatoes compared to some of the evil Max had faced. He would be able to keep Paige safe. No doubt about it. Hell, taking care of her would be his pleasure.

He watched as she leaned down and picked up a napkin off the floor. Man-o-man. His mouth went dry, his heart slammed in his chest, and blood pounded through his veins as it headed southward.

Sweet. Definitely sweet.

Yeah, protecting Paige would be his pleasure.

PAIGE'S HEART WAS RACING, her palms were sweating, and she could barely breathe. Had Brad found her again and sent yet another thug after her? She glanced at the table on the patio. The man was watching her.

When would this nightmare end? She was tired of running, tired of being frightened all the time. She didn't know who to trust and where to hide.

Her life used to be peaceful—boring, in fact. Get up. Go to work. Have dinner with Brad. Start it all over the next day.

Now she never knew if each day would be her last. Should she slip out the back and run away from the guy on the patio? She could head toward Miami, then on up the East Coast. Maybe to Savannah. Or Richmond.

Someplace far away from here.

Looking over her shoulder, she wasn't surprised to see the man was still watching her.

Leaving definitely seemed like the best idea, just in case Brad had sent him. Better safe than sorry.

Better safe than dead.

Of course, if the guy continued to watch her every move, slipping away was going to be hard. But she'd do it. She'd lost Brad and his goons before, and she could do it again.

Even if this guy didn't seem as dense as the others had been, she was fairly certain he was after her. Why else was he watching her so closely?

She glanced at him again and was surprised to see he was talking to a woman who'd pulled up a chair at the table next to his.

Doubt entered Paige's mind. The guy wasn't even looking at her. He seemed completely engrossed in his conversation with that woman.

Paige nibbled on her bottom lip. Did that mean he hadn't been sent by Brad after all? Or, did it mean he was merely trying to divert suspicion? Maybe he simply was what he claimed to be, a guy looking for a place to rent so he could start his new life.

Or, maybe, he planned on convincing her he was harmless only to turn around and attack her when she least suspected it.

The only thing she was sure of was that she no longer knew what to think about anything or anyone.

"Hey Paige, whatcha need?" Tim Maitland, the owner and lead bartender of the Sunset Café, tapped her on the shoulder. "You okay? I've been talking and you haven't heard a word I've said."

"Beer," Paige said, her gaze still on the man.

Tim followed her gaze and laughed. A tall, wiry man with thinning red hair and tiny glasses, Tim laughed often and loudly and had the wrinkles to prove it.

"Oooh. I see the problem," Tim said. "Major eye

Liz Jarrett   13

candy at three o'clock. Cute. Definitely cute." He let
out a whistle. "I like that whole macho-sexy thing he's
got going. No wonder you weren't listening to me. Emilio, check out this hunk."

Emilio Gonzales, Tim's partner and the restaurant's
head chef, leaned over the bar. "Definitely your type,
Tim-boy. Except I think he's straight. Sorry."

Tim's face crumpled. "He's not straight."

"He's looking at that lady's coconuts, something you
never do."

"Hey, I look at coconuts," Tim said, drawing out the
last word with emphasis. "Just not on ladies."

Both Emilio and Tim laughed at his joke, but Paige
could barely manage a smile.

"I need a beer," she told Tim once he had himself
somewhat under control.

Tim patted her hand. "Don't fret. I don't really think
he's interested in that woman, so you still have a shot
at him."

Paige shook her head. "It's not like that."

Tim rolled his eyes. "Pulease, sweetheart. Of course
it is. Much to my disappointment and Emilio's glee,
that man is horribly hetero. But that's good news for
you, and based on how yummy he is, that means he's
got your motor running. You lucky lady."

Paige didn't feel lucky at all. Far from it. She glanced
at man on the patio again, and this time, he was looking straight at her. When he noticed her watching him,
he winked. Paige felt another bead of sweat roll down
her back.

"He says he just got out of the Navy and is looking for a place to stay," Paige stated, still watching the man.

Tim set the beer on the counter, then leaned farther over so he could get a better look. "When Mr. Gorgeous mentioned he was looking for a place to stay, you did tell him you had a nice, comfy double bed in your apartment, didn't you?"

Stunned, Paige stared at Tim. "Of course not. I don't know that man." Even if she weren't afraid that Brad had sent him, she wouldn't invite a strange man home.

"Tim would have. Definitely in his younger days," Emilio said. "He used to have the morals of a junkyard dog."

Tim laughed and blew a loud kiss at the other man. "I love it when you flatter me."

Emilio turned so his back was to the other man. "For some of us, like you and me, sweet Paige, love is special. If what you feel for the handsome young man is special, I say go for it. If not, pass. He'll find what he needs with coconut woman."

Paige shook her head again. "I'm just trying to serve his beer, not—"

"Seduce him within an inch of his sanity," Tim blurted. "Got it, but frankly, too bad. He's tall, dark, mysterious, and built like a Greek god. Being a breathing female, you should be contemplating taking that boy on night maneuvers and doing some wild and wicked things with him between the sheets."

Paige frowned at Tim. "You need some serious therapy."

Tim laughed again and set a beer on the counter. "Tell me about it."

Emilio shrugged. "Paige, pet, if Tim weren't insane, how would the rest of us know we're just fine?"

Paige grabbed the beer and ignored their laughter. Those two were a mixed blessing. Since starting work here, they'd been absolute dolls to her, but they simply didn't understand what her life was like. It wasn't their fault. She'd never shared with them what was happening. She hadn't shared it with anyone.

How did you tell someone your ex-fiancé was trying to kill you? Not exactly something easily worked into a conversation.

Since there was no putting this off, Paige drew a calming breath into her lungs, picked up the beer, and headed back out to the patio. She didn't care if this guy liked men, women, or goats. She just wanted him as far away from her as possible.

Those directions she'd given him should do the trick.

This was so frustrating and frightening. What did Brad want from her? Okay, so she'd broken up with him. She couldn't believe that was worth chasing her halfway across the country.

When her tires had been slit, she'd figured he'd been releasing his anger.

Then her apartment had been broken into and ransacked. Again, everyone had said it was a coincidence.

But when a man had chased her through a mall parking lot, she'd known something was terribly wrong.

So she'd taken a trip to New York. Just to give Brad time to cool off. But she'd woken up to find someone trying to break into her hotel room. And when the police had arrived, the man had shot at them.

They'd shot back, but he'd gotten away. At that point, Paige knew she was in serious trouble. She'd talked to one police officer after another, and everyone insisted it was nothing but a random break-in. She'd desperately wanted to believe them, but deep down inside, she'd known they were wrong. She'd known something very bad was happening.

So she'd gone to stay at her grandmother's house in Connecticut. It was a small house in a small town with almost no crime. Still, she'd awoken to the screech of the alarm blaring in the middle of the night. Thankfully, the police had been there almost immediately. They claimed it was probably kids, but again, she'd known better.

She'd known beyond a doubt that for her own safety and the safety of the people she loved, she needed to disappear until she figured out what was going on and what to do about it.

That had been six months ago and she was still running. She just didn't know why.

"Here's your beer." She set the frosty glass in front of the man. This close, she could see how amazingly blue his eyes were and how thick his dark black hair was. It annoyed the heck out of her, but she felt her pulse rate pick up. Tim was right about one thing—the guy was incredibly handsome.

But he almost could be here to hurt her. Whatever he was, he didn't seem like a beach bum looking for a slow-lane lifestyle.

The guy smiled again, a slow, lazy smile that she bet won over a lot of women. "Thanks, Paige. I really appreciate it."

She stopped, fear washing over her. "How do you know my name?"

He leaned a little closer, so Paige instinctively took a step back.

"Those bartenders called you Paige. Right before the red-haired one called me eye candy." The man leaned back in his chair, his smile now a full-fledged grin. "By the way, my name is Max Walker. And as much as I'd like to visit your double bed, I think you're smart not to invite me."

Paige felt a flush climb her cheeks. "You heard—"

"Everything you all said. Might want to keep that in mind the next time you want to plot something. Everyone on the patio can hear you."

Frantically, Paige tried to remember what she'd said to Tim and Emilio. Had she mentioned she was afraid of Max? Had she said anything about Brad?

Scanning her memory, she was relieved to find that she hadn't. At least she hadn't lost her common sense along with her peace of mind.

"Thanks for the tip," was all she could think to say. "Good luck finding an apartment."

He nodded. "And a job. I'll need luck with that as well."

She turned to head back inside. "Enjoy your beer."

"Whoa, Paige."

She wanted nothing more at the moment than to get away from Max. Maybe he was who he said he was, but whoever he was, he disturbed her. At this point, she didn't want to be disturbed. She wanted peace and quiet in a world that didn't have potential bad guys who looked like they were sex gods.

Turning slowly, she tried to still her racing heart. "Yes?"

He pulled his wallet out of his jeans. "Want money?"

"Excuse me?"

"For the beer, Paige. Not for a tour of your double bed. How much for the beer?"

"Six dollars."

He let out a long, low whistle. "Man, life's expensive here." He handed her a ten. "Since Key West costs so much, keep the change. Bet you can use a little extra cash to make ends meet."

Paige looked at the ten in her hand, willing her breathing to slow, willing the fear that was choking her to subside.

"Paige, you okay?"

She glanced at Max. He was looking at her with concern. Great. This guy had to think she was crazy. Most days, even she thought she was crazy. Then she'd remember the alarm blaring at her grandmother's house and know she wasn't making this up.

"I'm fine," she told him and headed back inside. When she reached the bar, she told Tim and Emilio about the acoustic problem but they just laughed and waved at Max. Despite herself, Paige looked over at Max, too, only to find him once again engrossed in a conversation with the woman at the next table.

"You have much better coconuts," Tim said from behind Paige. "Don't despair."

Paige sighed, but despite herself, her gaze skimmed over Max Walker. He really was good-looking. Not to mention that he was built like he could take on the world. His dark black hair hit his collar and gave him an even rougher look.

But his eyes were what got to her. They were an amazingly dark, almost midnight-blue. He had a tough, rugged look about him, and she couldn't help thinking that if this guy really was out to get her, then she was in big trouble.

2

MAX LEANED BACK in his chair and watched Paige once again disappear behind the counter in the bar. All afternoon, she'd avoided him. Sure, she'd brought him another beer and his dinner when he'd ordered it, but other than that, she'd kept her distance.

She was suspicious of him. He knew it. So if he didn't want her to run, he needed to do something to make her trust him. In his experience, the only way to change someone's mind was to do the exact opposite of what they expected. As soon as she'd walked away this last time, he'd reviewed what he knew about Paige in his mind. She was rich. Probably a little spoiled. But not stupid.

Definitely not stupid. Okay, so she didn't know how to disappear so no one would find her. Not unusual. Most honest people didn't. But she'd feared for her safety, and she'd known enough to run.

No, Paige wasn't stupid, which meant there was a big chance she was going to run again.

That would be the smart move, but of course, that was the last thing he wanted. He wasn't about to chase her all over the country. He'd have to get her to stay put, then let her father know he'd found her.

So now, he had some soothing to do. He stood and wandered inside the bar. There was no sign of Paige, but based on what the skinny red-haired guy behind the bar was saying to someone back in the kitchen, she was taking her dinner break.

Max pulled up a bar stool and looked at the bartender.

"Know where I can find a job?" he asked.

The guy gave Max the once-over, then asked, "Know how to make a Blue Angel?"

Max resisted the temptation to smile. Instead he said flatly, "Blue Curaçao, Crème de Violettee, brandy, lemon juice and creme."

The guy leaned against the counter. "Grasshopper?"

"Vodka, Green Crème de Menthe, White Crème de Cacao."

"Singapore Sling?"

"Gin, cherry brandy, lemon juice, club soda, and powdered sugar."

"Naked Russian Sailor."

Max frowned at him. "Cute."

With a laugh, the man reached across the counter and shook Max's hand. "Hey, a guy can dream. The name's Tim, and if you can mix 'em the way you remember them, you've got a job. Come over to this side of the bar and show me what you can do."

Max headed to the other side. When he'd first gotten out of the Navy and hadn't joined the force yet, he'd mixed drinks one summer.

As he worked, he subtly pumped Tim for information about Paige. Not that it took any work. The guy was a regular volcano—once he got going, he spilled everything he knew about life in general and Paige in particular.

She worked two afternoon shifts and the night shift on the weekend. She'd started working there about three months ago. Tim knew she lived a couple of miles from the club, but he'd never been to her place. A dark-haired man named Emilio who was working in the kitchen hollered out that he'd been to her place and it was nice, which caused Tim to yell back that kitchen help was to be seen, not heard.

Max filled a couple of drink orders while the two men verbally sparred back and forth. Man, this was one crazy place. Even the crowd was odd. Beach bums, bathing beauties, gays, straights, families. Every imaginable group was here. All of them seemed to be having the time of their lives hanging out in a café decorated to look like something out of Robinson Crusoe.

After Tim finished his shouting match, he grinned at Max. "Some people. Anyway, like I was saying about Paige, lots of men hit on her. In fact, a couple of regulars hassle her almost every weekend. But she never goes out with any of them. Ever. Not because she has a boyfriend. If she did, I'm sure the guy would have stopped by. But no jealous boyfriend has ever appeared."

Tim narrowed his eyes in what Max had to assume the other man thought was a menacing look but actually was a little cross-eyed. "But you were checking out coconut woman, so you're not interested in Paige."

Okay, now Max was officially lost in this convoluted conversation. "Excuse me?"

"The chicapoo with the coconuts you were sizing up earlier," Emilio hollered from the kitchen. "One woman at a time, my man."

It took a couple of seconds for Max to realize the men were talking about the woman who'd sat at the table next to him. He'd only said a word or two to her as a way to distract Paige. He'd hardly noticed the woman, and certainly not her...er, um, coconuts.

"I was just being nice," he said to Tim, who made a snorting noise.

"I think Paige is getting over a bad relationship, so you steer clear if you're not sincere. Or else, you'll answer to me," Tim said.

"Me, too," came the response from the kitchen. "And my brothers. I have lots of brothers."

Max bit back a grin on that one. Instead he assured both men, "I'm not interested in hitting on Paige. I just want a job."

"Which you have," Tim said, slapping him hard on the back. "And I'm glad to hear you're not interested in Paige. She's just about the best waitress I've ever met, plus she helps me with the books. She even managed to set me up with a computer program and everything. The lady's amazing," Tim pronounced, leaning back against the counter and watching Max fill a drink order for a group of seven. "And you're a pretty good bartender. Guess I'm one lucky guy."

"You always hire people on the spot?" Max was amazed anyone in this day and age could still be trusting. "Seems dangerous."

"People lie on their applications, anyway," Tim said with a shrug. "So I go with my instincts. My instincts tell me you're on the level."

Max barely managed not to laugh. Him? On the level? Hardly.

"I appreciate the chance," was all he said.

And he did. This job was great cover. Now all he'd have to do was make sure his schedule lined up with Paige's. It would make watching her that much easier.

He'd made quite a few drinks and shot the breeze with Tim and Emilio for some time when Paige returned from her dinner break. As soon as she saw him behind the bar, she skittered to a stop.

"What are you doing?" she asked, the color draining from her face.

"Working." He wiped the bar, keeping his voice flat and neutral.

Her expression made it clear she'd rather be set on fire than have Max work at the Sunset Café. She turned to Tim. "Can I talk to you for a sec?"

Tim shrugged. "Sure. Talk. But make it quick. I want to go to dinner since Max has the bar."

Paige looked at Max and then back at Tim. "Alone. I'd like to speak to you alone."

Tim laughed. "Angel, I know you're having trouble resisting me, but like I keep telling you, I'm gay. Sorry."

Paige frowned. "I need to talk to you."

With a small bow, Tim teased, "A boss's job is never done. So what did you want to tell me?"

Max couldn't help feeling sorry for Paige. She obviously didn't want him here, but his job made it imperative that he stay. Knowing the best thing he could do was appear uninterested in her, he walked away.

Behind him, Max heard Tim ask Paige again what she wanted. Before she could answer, a tall Hispanic man wandered out from the kitchen. Emilio, Max assumed.

"I've had the best idea," Emilio announced to everyone in general. "I can't believe how amazing I am."

Tim groaned. "And you call me insane. Sounds to me like you're delusional."

"Ha, listen to my idea." Emilio paused, then spread his arms wide. "I say we have Paige and Max plan the Midsummer Night's Extravaganza this year."

Tim screamed and Max's hand flew to his belt where he normally carried his gun. Thankfully, no one seemed to notice since they were staring at Tim.

"That's brilliant," he told Emilio. "You're right. You are amazing."

Max looked at Paige, thinking she might have a clue what was happening. Personally he didn't like the sound of this. "Midsummer's Night Extravaganza?"

"Every July 15, we take over the parking lot and have a huge party," Emilio said. "It's a blast. We celebrate the best of a Key West summer."

Tim grinned, first at Max, then at Paige. "This year, you two get to plan it. Emilio and I will get back to you with details."

With that, the two men disappeared into the kitchen talking as they went about how brilliant they were. Max stared after them for a moment, then turned to look at Paige. She was flushed. He knew she was upset, so to take her mind off her troubles, he asked a question to which he already knew the answer.

"Do you know what they're talking about?"

She shook her head. "No. But I'm not sure we're going to like it."

"I'm *positive* we're not going to like it," he said. He wiped the counter a couple of times. He could feel her watching him, knew she was debating about him. When he finally glanced up, she quickly looked away.

"I really appreciate Tim giving me this job," he said. "But I was surprised he hired me on the spot. Does he do that a lot?"

Paige shrugged. "More often than not."

"Seems kind of risky," Max pointed out. "Do his instincts usually pay off?"

She looked him dead in the eyes. "Sometimes. I guess time will tell in your case."

Then she walked away, leaving Max smiling behind her.

PAIGE GLANCED AROUND, then unlocked the door to her apartment and turned off the alarm. Everything looked normal. Perfectly normal. No one jumped out from behind the sofa. No one was hiding in the kitchen. Her apartment hadn't been ransacked.

Maybe she was wrong and no one was stalking her. At least not anymore. Nothing unusual had happened since she'd come to Key West almost three months ago. Maybe her life really was getting back to normal. Surely he wasn't still chasing her after all this time. He had to have moved on.

Still, she hurried inside, relocked the door, and reset the alarm. Then whistled for Sugar. The dog came bounding out of the spare bedroom, her tail wagging like a windshield wiper in a bad storm.

Paige knelt and patted the mutt. Sugar didn't look like a guard dog. She looked friendly, a fluffy cloud of white fur. Paige had chosen her for that very reason. Sugar might not look tough, but she was. Paige hoped that if she got in trouble again, she'd be half as brave as Sugar was.

Paige finished patting the dog and headed toward the kitchen. She was tired. Really tired. Not because her shift at the Sunset Café had been difficult. But it had been troubling since she wasn't sure if the new guy Max was someone to fear or not.

This was no way to live. She was never sure who she could trust or if she was safe. Max seemed like a nice guy. Everyone at work liked him. But she didn't know if she could trust him. Heck, she didn't even know if she could trust anyone at the Sunset, which was why she'd never gotten close to her co-workers.

But living like this was wearing her down. She wanted friends. She wanted to trust people. She wanted her old life back.

Maybe the police had been right. Maybe all those incidents had just been a string of bad luck. Nothing suspicious had happened since she'd been in Key West. That had to mean something, didn't it?

She could call her father and ask him what he heard about Brad. After a second, she scratched that idea. Roger Delacourte wouldn't listen to her. He'd wanted her to marry Brad. He'd liked the idea of having a senator's son in the family, so she knew he'd say whatever it took to get her to come home.

Even if she could get hurt.

A tapping on the front door made Sugar growl softly. Instinct kicked in again. For one second, Paige remained motionless, and then the tapping formed the usual pattern—*tap, tap, tap-a-tap-tap.*

Diane Mitchell.

Letting out the breath she hadn't even realized she'd been holding, Paige headed to the front door and looked through the peephole. Sure enough, it was Diane, making goofy faces.

"Let me in. I've got man trouble," Diane said.

That made two of them.

After turning off the alarm, Paige undid the dead bolt, then opened the door. Before she'd even had a chance to say hello to her friend and neighbor, Diane burst into the room.

"I can't believe what Kyle has done now. I swear, I'm going to break up with him. I don't care how many years we've lived together, the man has got to go."

Paige shut and relocked the door, resetting the alarm. "What happened?"

Diane was a petite brunette who was constantly upset with her boyfriend. But after three months, Paige knew her friend would never actually break up with Kyle. The two were very much in love, even though they argued fairly often.

"He wants to buy a *house*," Diane said flatly as she flopped onto the couch. "Can you imagine?"

Baffled, Paige shrugged and sat in the chair facing the couch. "What's wrong with wanting to live in a house? Maybe he's tired of living in an apartment."

Diane looked like she'd suggested they live in a cave. "A house, Paige. In the *suburbs*. He wants us to leave the Keys and move to some suburb near Miami." Diane shuddered. "Old people live in houses in the suburbs. People with two-point-five kids live in houses. Artists don't. Creators don't."

Paige barely refrained from laughing. Diane wasn't technically an artist. She made paperweights out of shells and sold them to the tourists. Paige was fairly certain gluing three shells together and drawing a smile on them didn't count as art.

Still, she could tell Diane was upset. Truthfully, she

couldn't quite sympathize. Right now, a nice house somewhere safe sounded wonderful to Paige.

"Diane, maybe you two could compromise. You could buy a house, but not necessarily in the suburbs. Although, I think you're being too harsh. I'm sure lots of artists live in the suburbs."

Diane rolled her eyes and sat cross-legged. "Not if they want to maintain their edge. I can't create in a world like that, and Kyle knows it. It would *destroy* my life."

No, it wouldn't. As a person whose life had been destroyed, Paige knew that for a fact. Up until a few months ago, she'd worried about every little thing.

Now, she only worried about one thing—being safe.

"Yoo-hoo," Diane waved her hands. "You're not listening to me. You're going all serious."

Paige blinked. "Sorry."

For a couple of seconds, Diane just looked at her. Then she asked, "When are you going to tell me what's going on?" When Paige started to deny her assumption, Diane shook her head. "Don't tell me nothing's going on because I know that's not true. I can look at you and tell you've got something serious on your mind."

Paige appreciated Diane's concern but she was hesitant to tell anyone what had happened. More than likely, Diane would think she was crazy.

After all, didn't you have to be crazy to think a senator's son was hunting you? Besides, she had no proof.

Heck, she didn't even know for certain he was after her.

Maybe she really was crazy.

"Nothing is wrong," Paige said, standing and putting Sugar on her leash. "Want to go for a walk with us?"

She wasn't trying to chase off Diane, but she did want to change the subject. And Sugar needed to go out.

"Fine. Don't tell me what's bothering you. We'll talk about something else," Diane said, sighing dramatically. "But you remember, kiddo, if you ever need anything...anything at all, you come to me."

"I will," Paige said, meaning it. She appreciated knowing she had at least one friend in the world whom she could trust. Okay, maybe two. She trusted Tim. And Emilio. She trusted him, too.

Now that she thought about it, there were a couple of the waitresses at work, Krystal and Annie, who she trusted as well. They'd been nothing but sweet to her since the day she'd started at the Sunset.

Maybe she wasn't so alone after all.

Feeling infinitely better, she was tempted to talk to Diane not about Brad and the whole mess she'd left behind in Chicago, but about that guy, Max, who'd shown up at the café today.

But if she said one word about Max, Diane wouldn't understand her concerns. Instead she'd dig for details—was he cute, was he nice, did he want to come to dinner at Paige's apartment. She wouldn't understand that Paige didn't want to date the man, she just wanted to decide if she should be scared of him or not.

Diane headed toward the door. "Let's go for this walk and see if we can figure out my man trouble. Then maybe we can talk about finding a man for you. I think it's about time you had a little Y-chromosome action tossed your way."

Paige shook her head. "Y-chromosome action is the last thing I want, thank you very much."

"Ah, hon, don't be that way. They're not all dogs. Some of them are downright sweet," Diane reasoned. "It's like picking a mango. You have to look it over carefully, because sometimes it's difficult to see the rotten spots. But once you find a good one, grab it and hold on, because it's going to bring you a lot of happiness."

Paige laughed and headed toward the stairs. "Thanks for the tip. I'll be sure to remember that the next time I go shopping for a mango. And you should keep that in mind when you think about leaving Kyle. I'm pretty sure he's an excellent mango."

Diane got a sappy smile on her face. "Yes. Even with his nutso idea about a house, he's still an excellent mango. Now all we have to do is find you one."

Paige didn't bother to answer. Instead she headed down the stairs. She had no interest in finding a mango...rotten or not. Right now all she wanted was her life back.

MAX SLID DOWN in his seat when he saw Paige and another woman walk out of the apartment building. They had a dog with them and were engrossed in a conversation. For about ten minutes, they walked around the apartment building, never getting far from the entrance. Then, after the dog was done, they headed back inside.

Max sat up and pulled his cell phone out of his pocket. Time to let Trav know he'd found Paige.

Travis answered on the first ring. "Hey, you're late. You were supposed to check in at ten your time."

"I had to work," Max explained. "My shift didn't end until a few minutes ago."

"What are you talking about? What shift? Did you find Alyssa Delacourte or not?"

Max didn't miss the frustration in Travis's voice. "Yeah. I found her." He explained about the Sunset Café and his new job. "Now I'm sitting in my car outside her apartment."

"You call her father yet?" Trav rustled through some papers. "Want the number again?"

Max started to say he had the number and would make the call in a couple of minutes but something stopped him. Something told him that was a bad decision. He'd learned over the years to go with his gut on things like this. Maybe that was why he'd never lost a client.

"You call him. Tell him I've found her but I didn't tell you where I am," Max said.

"Mind telling me why all the cloak-and-dagger? I thought Roger Delacourte was positive the danger was over. He's not going to be happy if I don't tell him where his daughter is."

"Then say she's in Atlanta. Give him Paige's old address," Max said.

"Paige?"

"That's what Alyssa goes by. She calls herself Paige Harris." After a second, he told his brother, "Don't tell Delacourte that, either."

"I take it you don't trust her father," Travis said dryly. "Why else wouldn't you tell the client what he was paying you to find out?"

Max wasn't sure why he didn't want to let Paige's father know where she was, he just didn't. Something didn't feel right. "Let me scope this out first."

Travis laughed. "Is she cute? Is that it? You want to spend some time with her before you convince her to go home to Daddy?"

Leave it to Travis to come up with a lame theory like that. Max told his brother in no uncertain terms what he thought of that idea, but Travis only laughed more.

"Fine, fine, I stand corrected. Your motives are pure. But then why all the secrets? The NYPD said that guy who was trying to break into her hotel room was some two-bit thief who had a long history of robbery. He had no connection to Collier. He wasn't a hit man sent to kill her. Just some petty crook."

Yeah, that might be true, but Max still couldn't shake the feeling that Paige was in real danger. "Let me have a few more days to check this out."

"Whatever," Travis said. "I'll call the father. Take

the heat for you. Suffer through his anger. Be your fall guy."

Max groaned. "Gee, what a sport. Just remember, I gave you a job when no one else would."

"Hey, buddy, I saved your butt when you couldn't find anyone decent to work for you," Travis countered in their familiar joke.

"That only proves I still don't have any decent help," Max added dryly.

"Ha. Very funny."

"So how are things at the office?" Max asked.

"Fine. I caught up all your paperwork for you," Travis said. "Did all your boring tasks. Cleaned up the filing. You know, stuff we kid brothers always have to do for our older brothers who can't be bothered."

"Put it on my tab. Let's see, by my calculations, I owe you three million, six hundred and fifty-three thousand for the times you saved my butt, and you owe me four million, seven hundred and thirty-six thousand for all the times I've saved yours. I'm still winning."

Travis laughed. "Sounds about right."

"Anything else new?"

"We did land a client," Travis said. "HRM Advertising thinks their accountant is embezzling from them. Wants me to check the guy out."

"Sounds exciting," Max said. "Make sure you wear a bulletproof vest at all times."

"Yeah, well not all of us are lucky enough to get damsels in distress to protect. Some of us actually have to work for a living."

Max laughed, then told his brother, "Hey, thanks."

Max knew his younger brother understood exactly what he meant. They'd grown up as Army brats with a strict father and a mother who walked away when they were tiny. For as long as he could remember, it had been the two of them taking on the world and covering each other's back.

He'd do anything for Travis, and he knew his brother felt the same.

"CYA, bro," Travis said. "CYA."

"Will do. You, too." With that, Max hung up and settled back in his seat. Yeah, he'd take care of himself. He'd also take care of Paige. After all, he had his perfect record to protect—he'd never lost a client.

And he never would.

3

"COME ON, BABY, it's not going to kill you. Just one kiss. That's all I want. I'll give you a big tip." With a wink, the man added, "If you're really good, I'll give you more than just the tip."

The man and his friends laughed. Paige turned and headed back inside to get their beers. If they were this obnoxious and they hadn't even had a beer yet, what were they going to be like after a couple of drinks?

Jerks.

When she reached the bar, she told Max the order, then rubbed her temples. Her head hurt. Badly. And she was practically dead on her feet. She'd gotten hardly any sleep the last couple of nights. It had been windy, and she'd kept hearing noises outside.

"You okay?" Max asked when he set the beers in front of her. "Got a headache?"

"A little."

"Want some aspirin?"

"Maybe later." Paige looked at him. Max had been working at the Sunset Café a little over a week. She had to admit, he seemed like a nice guy. He didn't hit on her or make dirty cracks around her. In fact, he rarely talked to her other than to discuss drink orders.

That was why he surprised her when he said, "We need to talk."

"About?"

"That thing Tim and Emilio want us to plan. They grabbed me earlier tonight and it looks like they're not letting it go."

Oh. That. She'd forgotten all about it. "Are they really serious about this?"

Max didn't seem any happier about it than she was. "'Fraid so. Guess we can talk later tonight."

With that, Max went back to tending bar. Paige had to admit, she liked him. She no longer believed Brad had sent him. He hardly seemed to notice her most of the time.

But Max was good to have around. He was friendly to the customers and firm with the ones who had had too much to drink.

Plus, no one argued with Max when he took their keys away and called a cab instead of letting them drive. Like Tim said, who would argue with Max? The man looked like he could bench-press a Buick.

Taking a deep breath, Paige headed back to the jerk's table. She kept her distance from him, putting the drinks down quickly, and then backing away. Unfortunately, while she'd been working, she hadn't realized the man had stood and circled the table. Now, as she went to walk away, he blocked her path.

"How about that kiss?" He reached out and grabbed her arm. "Chad wants a nice, long, wet one. Come on, baby. Just one kiss."

Paige yanked her arm free. She should have seen this coming. If she hadn't been so tired, she would have been thinking clearer.

"Keep your hands off me," she told the man firmly, wiping the spot where he'd touched her.

The man lunged again, catching her arm before she could move away. He leaned closer so his face was even with hers, then asked, "Or what? What *you* going to do, sweet thing?"

"I don't know what she'll do, but I'll rip your head off," a deep voice said flatly. "So I'd let her go if I were you."

The man looked up, then seeing Max, dropped Paige's arm immediately. She got a lot of satisfaction watching his face turn a pasty-white. Slowly he moved back to his side of the table.

"Hey, I'm not looking for trouble," the man said, pulling out his chair. "But the lady's been coming on to me all night. And a guy can only be pushed so far."

"You're a liar," Max said. "Now pack up and get out of here. And make sure you pay for those drinks."

Max folded his arms across his chest. He really did look like a mountain at the moment, and she knew with absolute certainty that Max was a guy who knew how to take care of himself.

The weasel obviously knew it, too, because he was so nervous he was sweating. Good. He deserved to sweat.

Max glanced at her. "You okay?"

She nodded and tried to smile. "Yes. Thanks."

"No problem."

The guy started to mouth off again, but Max turned his attention back to the group, and they fell silent. The man and his friends stood, tossed some money on the table, and headed toward the door.

On his way by, the man said softly to Paige, "This isn't over, sweet thing."

Max made a growling sound, which sent the man hurrying out like a scared rabbit.

"What an ass," Max muttered, shaking his head. "Some guys don't have a clue. If you want, I can teach you some self-defense moves to help out in cases like this."

Paige released a shaky breath. "That would be great," she said. "I'd appreciate it."

"Sure, no problem. You sure you're okay?" Max asked.

Paige ran her hands through her hair then lowered them to her sides. "I'm fine. Thanks for..." She sighed. "Coming to my rescue."

Max patted her on the shoulder. "I'm sure you could have handled them on your own. I just figured I'd give you a hand because you have a headache. Speaking of hands—" He reached out and lifted one of her hands. He ran his thumb several times across the back of her hand in a gesture he probably thought was soothing. "Your hands are shaking."

Well, if they weren't before, they sure were now. Unexpectedly, Paige found his touch incredibly arousing. In the back of her mind, she knew everyone in the Sunset was watching them. Warm breeze caressed her skin, tropical music drifted down from the overhead speakers.

And yet, all she could focus on was Max. She stared at him as he gently rubbed her hand. "What are you doing?"

"Like I said, you're shaking," he pointed out. "I'm trying to calm you down."

Um, then this wasn't the way. It was like throwing gasoline on a fire. Rather than calming her, his touch was awaking desires she'd buried long ago. He was making it difficult for her to breathe, impossible for her to think. She wanted to pull away from him, wanted to tell him to stop, but lust had wrapped her in its web.

How could this be happening? A few minutes ago, she'd been angry and scared. Now she was more turned on than she'd ever been in her life.

What she was feeling must have shown clearly on her face because after a second, Max's expression changed. For one heartbeat, he stopped rubbing her hand and just looked at her. She could feel awareness surround them, and desire dance between them. He knew what she was feeling, and as she watched, she saw answering passion ignite and then burn hotly in his gaze.

He wanted her every bit as much as she wanted him.

Slowly, deliberately, he started caressing her hand again, this time his touch deliberately sensual. Paige felt heat seep through her body, and her gaze tangled with his as Max moved closer.

"Danger does this sometimes," he said, his voice soft and deep. "It doesn't mean anything, Paige. You're upset. That's what's causing this reaction."

She knew what he was saying, what he was trying to tell her, but his logical explanation did nothing to calm her racing heart.

"If that's true, then why are you feeling it, too?" she asked. "You weren't afraid."

He caressed her hand one last, lingering time, and then he slowly released her. With a small smile, he said, "'Cause I'm a guy. We're all animals, haven't you heard?"

With that, he headed back to the other side of the bar. Paige watched him walk away and tried to get her heartbeat to slow. The silence that had surrounded them abruptly evaporated. Everyone in the Sunset seemed to talk at once, and Paige knew they were talking about her. And Max. But she couldn't focus on them. Instead she was watching him.

He was wrong. He wasn't an animal. An animal would have taken advantage of what she'd been feeling. But Max hadn't. Even though she knew he'd felt the same punch of desire she'd felt, he'd walked away.

He wasn't an animal at all.

MAX SENSED DANGER. Serious danger. Hell, he more than sensed it—he saw danger. Sitting across the table from him. He and Paige were in jeopardy, and there didn't seem to be anything he could do about it.

Of all the times not to be armed.

"This extravaganza is the most important event the Sunset does each year," Tim said, grinning at Max and Paige. "It's a huge honor that Emilio and I are asking you to plan it."

Max barely managed to not say "bull." This wasn't an honor. It was off-loading work and they all knew it. He didn't want to do this, didn't even want to be in this meeting. But since Paige was here, he was here.

"It's not something I'm good at," he said, hoping Tim would get the clue and drop this nonsense. "In fact, I'll stink at it, so you should find someone else."

"It's because of the *extravaganza* part," Emilio said, nudging Tim. "He isn't the type of guy to use a word like that."

They both gave Max sympathetic looks, and he sighed. "Look, I don't care what you call the thing, it isn't something I do. I tend bar. That's what I do."

"We'll call it a festival," Tim said, ignoring everything Max had just said. "That's a nice manly word. Something he can say without trouble."

Max was all set to protest that it didn't matter to him what they called it, when Paige cleared her throat.

"I don't think it's something I'm interested in doing, either," she said. "Sorry."

Yes! An ally. Max turned and flashed her a thank-you grin. "See, neither of us wants to do it. I bet you can find someone else."

Tim hooted a laugh. "You're funny, Max. It's almost like you think we're asking." He looked at Emilio. "See, I hired these two with very little, no make that nothing, in the way of references." He grinned at Paige and Max. "Any of this ring a bell?"

Emilio grinned at them, too, and Max had to admit, these two had a real career ahead of them as con men if they wanted one. This was serious blackmail, and everyone in the room knew it.

"I do believe he and Paige aren't getting this," Emilio said. "Perhaps if you speak slower, Tim, they'll catch on."

Yeah, well Max for one was getting it now. "I was hired as a bartender."

"Look at your job description. You're a customer facilitator. That means you help guests have fun," Tim said.

Emilio nodded. "It's all about the customers. But don't pout, you two will be paid very well for doing this and you'll get time off your shifts. You'll have a blast. Every year, the employees beg us to pick them to do this. But we picked the two of you."

"Because?" Max had to ask.

"Because you two will bring something different to this," Tim said, his grin almost too big for his face. "I know it. Emilio knows it. You're not going to make this a typical Midsummer Night's Extravaganza—oops, make that Festival. See, it's already different. It's a festival."

He said the last part with a flourish, and Max seriously doubted a festival was one bit better than an extravaganza. Personally he'd rather take a bullet than do either one.

"I don't think—" he started at the same time Paige said, "Fine. I'll do it."

He shut his mouth. Well, that settled that. He really no longer had a choice. If he wanted to keep Paige in sight, he'd need to do this, too.

Well, hell.

"Fine," he said.

Tim grinned. "Terrific. Now the only guidelines are there are no guidelines. I have pictures of the ones from the past three years to get you started."

"Then it's all up to you," Emilio said. "Feel free to dazzle us."

Oh, yeah. That was going to happen.

"Remember, this sort of thing looks great on a résumé," Tim added with a wink.

Max had serious doubts this particular activity was going help him land his next client.

But he'd do it to keep this client safe.

He leaned back in his chair. Man, things weren't going well on this case. Not at all. First, he'd been hit with a punch of lust when he'd touched Paige's hand earlier tonight. Talk about a dangerous situation. He took his job seriously, and a serious investigator didn't get involved with a client.

And now he had to work on this stupid festival thing.

This night just kept going downhill faster than an out-of-control skier.

"I'm so glad the two of you agreed to do this," Emilio said. "I know it will be great. And you two will truly enjoy the experience."

Max glanced at Paige. She didn't look any happier than he felt.

"We'll try our best," she said. "Because, Tim, I do appreciate you giving me this job."

Tim looked like a cat with a canary in its mouth. "You're welcome." He looked at Max and raised one eyebrow.

"Fine. I appreciate the job, too," Max muttered. "And we'll try."

Tim laughed. "Hey, that's what I like. Enthusiasm. Okay, Emilio and I will settle for that. You two will try. That's good enough for us."

Max hoped it was because he wasn't going to spend any serious thought on this festival thing. He had more important things to do—mainly keeping Paige safe.

His only regret was he hadn't been able to protect her from Tim and Emilio and this plan of theirs.

PAIGE HAD NO IDEA why she'd said yes. Okay, maybe that wasn't quite true. Tim and Emilio had backed her into a corner, but even with that, they were her friends. They'd been good to her since she'd moved to Key West. It seemed to mean so much to them, and it didn't matter a bit to her.

Plus, maybe they were right. Maybe it would be fun. She could use a little fun in her life right now. Any distraction was welcomed.

"I think this is crazy," Max said as they left the back room.

She knew he wasn't happy about this, and couldn't help wondering why he'd agreed. Maybe he was afraid Tim really would fire him if he said no.

"Tim isn't unreasonable," she told him. "If you really don't want to do this, tell him no. He won't fire you."

Max's expression made it clear he didn't believe her. Paige knew he needed this job, so she felt badly about this.

"Seriously, just tell him no," she said.

With a shake of his head, Max headed back to the bar. Paige watched him start closing up for the night. He was an unusual person. Very focused. Very professional.

Very sexy.

She still couldn't believe the sensations that had washed over her earlier tonight when he'd touched her hand. She hadn't felt that intense burn of attraction in...maybe forever.

So why now? And why with this man?

It didn't make any sense.

Of course, what in her life right now did make sense?

She quickly finished up for the night, then headed out to the parking lot. This was the time of day she hated the most. The darkness. The drive home. The fear that made her heart race.

As always, she walked out with some of the other

employees. A group was good. There was safety in a group. Thankfully, the large parking lot was well lit, but she still stayed close to the others. But as she got closer to her car, she realized something was seriously wrong.

"My tire," she said, stopping. Her left front tire was completely flat.

"Wow, Paige, you've got a flat," said Krystal, one of the other waitresses. "Emilio, Max, fix Paige's car."

Paige walked slowly up to her car. A flat. Was it an accident? Or had that creep tonight come out to the parking lot and done this?

Worse, had Brad done this?

She spun around, scanning the parking lot, and almost bumped into Max. He'd obviously heard Krystal and had come over to help.

"I'll change it," Max hollered at Emilio and waved the other man away. Then, he knelt next to the tire and spent a lot of time looking it over. "Probably caught a nail," he finally said.

"Are you sure?" she had to ask. "I mean that guy tonight said he was going to do something."

Rather than looking at her like she was crazy, Max seemed to really consider her question. "It doesn't look like the air was let out, but I can't be sure. Still, how would that guy know which car was yours?"

He had a good point, but Paige still couldn't shake the feeling this was more than bad luck.

"I can change my own tire," she said, heading toward the trunk. She hated making this man come to her rescue twice in one night. How pathetic could she be?

"Haven't you been listening to Tim and Emilio," Max said, following her to the back of her car. "According to them, I've got hetero issues and can't say words like extravaganza. If that's true, then you know there's no way a macho beast like me is going to let you change your own tire. It could cause me serious psychological harm."

He said all this nonsense with such a straight face that Paige had to laugh. "Why don't I believe that?"

With a loud, silly sigh, he said, "Can we afford to risk it?"

Paige laughed again, and the panic that had been gnawing at her backed down. She knew as long as Max was here, she'd be safe. She knew that as surely as she knew her own name.

She unlocked the trunk of her car, and Max stood to lift out the spare. But he stopped and shook his head.

"Your spare is flat, too," he said, setting the tire back in the trunk. "You're a lady without a lot of hot air," he teased.

Looking at the spare, Paige had to admit, it made her feel better. The tires on this old clunker she'd bought when she moved here were awful. Chances were, the flat tonight was just bad luck.

Of course, now she had an even bigger problem—how to get home.

Max must have read her mind, because he said, "I'll

give you a lift home tonight. Then tomorrow we can get your car fixed."

Paige hesitated out of habit, then took a deep breath. She could trust Max. She was positive of that. Plus, everyone else had already left. She didn't have any other option.

"If it helps, I can swear on my brother's head that I'm a nice guy," he said when she didn't answer right away.

A bubble of laughter slipped out of Paige. "Swear on your brother's head?"

After a self-deprecating laugh, Max explained, "Yeah, it's something we started as kids. For some reason, we thought it made our promises sound official and that people would know they could trust us."

The image of a young Max and this unknown brother developing an elaborate plan delighted Paige. She'd never had a brother or sister, but she'd like to think they would have joined forces like Max and his brother had.

"Well, since you're swearing on your brother's head, how can I not accept a ride?" she teased. "Your car is the black sedan, right?"

He seemed surprised that she knew which car was his. "How'd you know?"

"I've seen you arrive at work," she said, trying to keep her voice neutral. Idiot. Why didn't she come out and say, you're cute and I couldn't help noticing you whenever you showed up?

Jeez. Talk about immature.

"Ah," was thankfully all he said. If he suspected her real motivation, he didn't comment on it. Instead he led the way to his car and unlocked the passenger side.

"This car suits you," she said as she slipped into the seat and glanced around.

Max frowned and was still frowning as he crossed to the driver's side and climbed in.

"Something wrong?" she asked.

"It's just that I don't think this car suits me," he finally said.

She bit back a smile. Oh. A guy thing. "Then why did you buy it?"

"It was cheap," he said.

"What kind of car do you think suits you?"

He immediately answered. "A low, red sports car. A Corvette. *That* suits me."

"Then I take it back. This car doesn't suit you at all, and the second you can get that sports car, you really should," she told him trying to keep the humor out of her voice, but not managing to accomplish it in the least. "In the meantime, you'll have to suffer."

To his credit, he laughed. "I guess Tim and Emilio aren't so wrong about me after all. I do have some bonehead macho guy issues."

"Naw. Just because you want to drive a sports car doesn't mean you're beyond redemption."

He laughed again. "Gee, thanks. Now I can sleep at night. So where to?"

"My apartment," she said, settling back in her seat.

"Got a Ouija board on you so I can get directions?"

"Sorry," she said, feeling once again like an idiot. It was funny, she felt so comfortable with Max that she almost assumed he knew where she lived.

"Go to the light and turn right," she told him.

"Then?"

"We'll take it a step at a time," she said, since she hated it when people gave her convoluted directions and expected her to remember them.

He started the car. "Probably a good idea. Macho Neanderthals are known for their retention problems."

Paige laughed again. She couldn't believe how relaxed she felt. How happy. It felt amazing.

As he drove, she carefully doled out directions to her apartment, laughing more as he pretended to get confused a couple of times.

"So tell me about this infamous brother on whose head you swear," she prompted when they had several blocks to go with no turns.

"Travis," he said. "Child of Satan to those of us who knew him when."

"Ouch. Bad kid growing up?"

"Just a handful."

The way he said that made Paige suspect he'd been the one to take care of Travis. "Did you raise him?"

After a noticeable hesitation, he said, "Promise you won't say *awww*."

"What?"

"If I tell you about Trav and me, promise you won't do that thing women do when they go '*awww*, that's so cute.'"

Paige couldn't help smiling in the darkness of the car. "No way. I'm not about to make a promise like that."

"Then my secret will remain a mystery."

When she realized he really wasn't going to tell her, she said, "Fine. I won't say *awww*."

"Better swear on my brother's head, just to be sure."

Paige laughed. "Fine. I swear on your brother's head I won't say *awww*. So what is this story?"

"Trav and me in a nutshell—Army brats. Busy dad. Mom long gone. Best friends. Watched each other's backs. Still close."

The *awww* hovered on Paige's lips, wanting to slip out, but she slammed her lips closed. A promise was a promise.

Still, with just those few words, Max had told her volumes about himself. And the fact that he was so nonchalant about it told her even more. His relationship with his brother was not only close, but it was vitally important to him.

She really admired Max.

"I didn't say *awww*," she pointed out finally.

"But you wanted to," he countered with a laugh.

"Yes, yes, I did. It's very sweet."

"Sweet is almost as bad as *awww*," he told her, stopping at a light. "But I'll let it slide. Which way now?"

"Left."

After he made the turn, she asked, "So if your father was Army, how'd you end up Navy?"

He laughed. "Connect the dots on that one, Paige.

Trav and I weren't thrilled with the Army, but we did like the service. So we chose Navy."

She knew there was so very much more to this story than he was telling her, but he'd already shared so much. More than she felt he wanted to share. And she appreciated his confidence. It made her feel very close to a man who up until tonight she'd hardly known.

Unable to resist, she said, "I get the feeling my dad is a lot like your dad."

"In what way?"

"Unreasonable expectations," she admitted, not only to him, but in a way, to herself. She'd always thought of her father as pushy and domineering, but now that she voiced her thoughts, she realized they were true. His expectations for her were unreasonable.

"Glad to hear you realize that," he said. "And at the risk of you calling me sweet again, I'll add that you need to remember, it's your game, Paige. You control the ball."

"Um, Max, that's good advice, but it won't make me call you sweet. It will, however, make me point out that that's a real macho kind of guy thing to say."

He chuckled. "What can I say? I admit it. It's who I am. Now quick, tell me the rest of the directions to your place before I become even more of a Neanderthal and am unable to communicate with anything other than grunts and groans and burps."

4

MAX HADN'T A CLUE why he'd told Paige that stuff about Travis, but he wasn't sorry he had. He liked the way she kept laughing, kept talking to him. He knew she trusted him, which of course, was good for the case. But that wasn't why he'd told her those things.

He'd told her those things because he'd wanted to tell her. He liked talking to Paige. Liked being around her.

Man, he was one dumb jerk.

When they pulled up in front of her apartment building, he found a spot and parked.

"Nice place," he said, studying it, pretending he hadn't spent the last several nights watching this very building from across the street. "You like living here?"

"It's quiet." She unbuckled her seat belt and pushed open the door. "Thanks for the ride. I appreciate it."

"No problem." Right before she shut the door, he asked, "Want me to walk you home?"

When she hesitated, he added, "Oh, come on. Give me a chance to do one noble thing tonight. I seriously can't leave you thinking of me as a caveman."

His silliness did what he'd hoped it would do. It made her smile. In the light from the interior of the car, he saw the tension she felt seep from her. "But I'm already home."

"I meant, do you want me to walk you to your door?"

"It's just up the stairs," she said, not really answering his question. "Besides, I didn't think Neanderthals went in for that type of thing."

He chuckled. "Like I said, I'm trying to reform. So I'm walking you, but just so you know, I can't stay. I need to go to the grocery store tonight or I'm going to be eating dust bunnies for breakfast."

Max undid his own seat belt and climbed out of the car. As he joined Paige, she asked, "You're going to the grocery store at two in the morning?"

"Sure. It's open 24/7. Two in the morning is a great time to shop. I have the whole store to myself. Makes it a lot easier to find all the bargains."

Even though it was too dark for him to see her face clearly, he could sense her smiling. "You're a bargain shopper?" she asked. "I had no idea."

"Always watching my pennies." He waited for her to precede him up the stairs. As she walked by, the faint scent of citrus surrounded him. It was too light to be perfume. More than likely it was the shampoo or soap she used.

He liked the smell. It was clean and fresh and suited her, but he sure wished he'd stop noticing these things. It wasn't making this assignment any easier. Why couldn't she be some mean hag with bad breath? Then he'd be able to concentrate.

But no, he had to get someone nice and cute. Life wasn't fair.

"I really appreciate the ride home," Paige said as she walked up the stairs.

Max would have answered, but watching the sexy way she moved temporarily distracted him. Man, he needed to get himself under control. He willed his libido to stop running wild. He was just walking her to the door. So what if the gentle sway of her hips as she climbed the stairs was driving him crazy? What difference did it make if the sexy scent of the soap she used made him want to howl with desire?

He was on a case. He was only here because he wanted to make certain Paige was safe. This was a job. Nothing more.

Get a grip.

"Ta da," Paige said, waving at a door. "I'm home safe and sound."

"Maybe I should check inside. Just to make sure," Max said, grateful for something else to focus on other than Paige's sexy walk. He took the key she handed to him and opened the door for her. Reaching inside, he switched on the overhead light. He scanned the living room. Everything looked fine. He could hear a dog barking somewhere inside the apartment. Must be that little fluff ball she took walking every night. Normally he thought it was great when clients had dogs to help protect them, but he wasn't sure the little prissy dog Paige had could scare off a squirrel, let alone some thug.

Paige nodded at the room. "See? Everything's fine."

Max looked down at her to tell her he wanted to check the other rooms, but the words evaporated when lust slammed into him. He told himself to walk away, to get the hell out of here before he did something stupid, but his brain seemed to have shut down. She was looking at him with so much emotion in her eyes, so much...*belief* that it made it hard to look away. He could easily tell she trusted him and that she liked him.

And damn it all, that she wanted him every bit as much as he wanted her. When her gaze fastened to his lips, he groaned.

"I gotta go," he said, scrambling for some semblance of professionalism. Without waiting for her comment, he headed for the stairs. He knew she was watching him, but he didn't turn around. Instead he headed back to his car like his life depended on it.

Because when it came right down to it, Paige's life did depend on him, and he wasn't about to lose sight of that no matter how much he might want her. He was going to keep his mind on this case and his fly zipped.

Even if it drove him crazy in the process.

PAIGE WAS FILLING the saltshakers when the sound of Emilio's laughter caught her attention. She leaned slightly to the right so she could see out onto the patio. Max was talking to Emilio, and based on the frown on Max's face, they were talking about the festival.

Poor guy. Paige really did feel for him. She knew

Max hated the idea of working on it. Maybe if she talked to Tim, he'd reconsider.

Another burst of laughter came from Emilio and Paige admitted Max was doomed. They'd just have to make the best of this situation.

Not that she minded. She liked the idea of spending time with him. She liked it a lot.

Probably too much. She had other things to think about now, other things to focus on. She couldn't allow herself to be distracted by a man, couldn't allow herself to pretend her life was normal. Sure, nothing had happened in the last three months, but that didn't mean she could let her guard down.

Did it?

Picking up another saltshaker, she started filling it. She could hear the deep tone of Max's voice as he talked to Emilio, and she had to admit, Max had an amazing voice. It was one of the first things she'd noticed about him. That and his blue eyes. And his hair. Max had great hair.

And a really, really great smile.

"Interesting technique," Tim said with a laugh. "Not my style, but interesting."

Paige jumped. She'd been so wrapped up in her inventory of things she liked about Max, she hadn't even heard Tim walk up.

She turned and looked at him, at a total loss as to what he meant. "What?"

He scratched his chin and nodded at the table. "Personally, I pour the salt *into* the shaker. But you may be on to something here. Let's toss out those antiquated shakers. People can simply scoop salt off the table."

Paige blinked, then with a sinking feeling looked down. Oh, for crying out loud. She'd been so busy thinking about Max that she'd completely missed the shaker and gotten salt all over the table.

"Sorry," she muttered, setting the shaker and salt container down. Quickly she brushed the spilt salt into her palm. "I'll clean this up right now."

"Don't forget to toss some over your shoulder for good luck."

At the sound of Emilio's voice, Paige looked up. At some point, he and Max had walked inside. Max was watching her, and when she looked at him, he grinned his trademark sexy grin that always managed to turn her insides to mush.

He definitely had an amazing smile.

"Toss some salt over your left shoulder," Emilio said, coming to stand next to Paige. "That's how you get good luck." He nudged Paige. "Don't you want some good luck?"

Sure, she wanted good luck. A truckload of good luck would come in handy right now. She found her gaze drifting back to Max, who was leaning against the bar, watching her. He raised one brow in question, and she felt her pulse rate pick up.

"It really works," Krystal said. "I spilt salt last Tuesday and when I got home, my husband had found a new job."

Annie, one of the other waitresses, came over to join

them. "I won twenty dollars in the lottery one time the day after I spilt some salt." She grinned at Paige. "You're so lucky to have spilt that. You're bound to have something great happen to you soon."

Tim laughed. "Paige, with these kind of testimonials, how can you resist? Toss the salt, honey, but toss it quickly because we open in ten minutes, and I want to get these tables done. So grab some salt, make a wish—"

"You don't make a wish," Emilio interjected, shaking his head. "Not when you toss salt. That's not how it works. Salt brings you good luck in general, not a specific wish."

"That's true," Annie added. "You don't make a wish."

Krystal bobbed her head. "Tim, you've got this all wrong. That's not how salt works."

Tim sighed and waved his hands in dismissal. "Then what good is it? A specific wish is much better than general good luck. What kind of superstition is this?"

"The kind of superstition that comes true," Emilio said, leaning toward Paige. "It worked for me. I spilt some salt last week, and I tossed it over my left shoulder. When I was doing laundry that night, I found a twenty in my jeans I didn't even know I had."

"Of course you knew you had that twenty," Tim said. "You borrowed it from me that afternoon."

"And because I found it, I was able to pay you back," Emilio said, rolling his eyes. "Stay with me here, Tim. I'm trying to make a point."

Tim laughed. "You're nowhere near making a point."

Emilio turned to Paige. "Trust me. Seize the day. Toss the salt."

Okay, now this was getting downright silly. Paige laughed. "Fine, fine. I'll toss the salt if it will make everyone happy."

Although she could certainly use the luck, she figured she was more likely to win the lottery without a ticket than get good luck out of this. Still, they were all looking at her, so trying to keep a straight face, she grabbed a pinch of salt and tossed it over her left shoulder. Looking at Emilio, she said, "All set."

The man grinned. "Now just sit back and wait for good luck to find you. And trust me, it will."

She could only hope so.

"Hey, Max, you want in on this salt thing?" Tim asked. "Paige spilt enough for the entire bar to get good luck."

"Tim, it doesn't work that way," Emilio said, brushing the rest of the salt into his palm. "You can't throw another person's salt. That would bring you *bad* luck. You don't mess with luck. Something bad could happen."

Muttering and shaking his head, Emilio headed across the bar and tossed the salt in the garbage can. "You don't mess with luck," he repeated before disappearing into the kitchen.

For a second, no one said a word. Then Tim said

dryly, "Anyone besides me pick up on the vibe that you don't mess with luck?"

Everyone laughed, and Paige couldn't help wishing this were real. That she was just one of the employees, laughing over a joke, and hanging with friends. A pang ran through her at the need for a normal life again.

Her gaze drifted to Max. She couldn't help wishing that was normal, too. That he could simply be a man she liked. Someone she'd like to get to know a lot better without worrying about Brad.

She glanced at the small dab of salt still in her hand. Unable to resist, she took another pinch and subtly tossed it over her shoulder. A little extra luck never hurt anyone.

And it certainly wouldn't hurt her.

MAX LOOKED AROUND the restaurant and wondered what he'd gotten himself into. Sure, he'd offered to teach Paige some self-defense techniques, but before he'd had a chance to say a word, Tim and Emilio had asked him to teach what he knew to all the employees of the Sunset Café.

He glanced at Paige, who was standing between Annie and Krystal. She looked exceptionally sexy today in her short red shorts and red-and-white T-shirt. She kept smiling at him, and each time she did, Max felt desire shoot through him. He had to admit, maybe teaching this class to all the employees would work in his favor. The last thing he needed at the moment was to be alone with Paige, but he did want her to learn a few things about protecting herself.

Especially now. Trav had told him last night that Paige's old apartment had been broken into after he'd told her father she was there. Either the old man was part of this or he'd told Brad Collier what Travis had said.

Either way, Max was now positive Paige was still in serious danger.

"I think we all agree this is nice of Max to teach us these techniques," Tim said to the assembled group. "We want to avoid being victims. Since he had a lot of training in the Navy, Max will give us an overview of the basics. I've asked him to teach these short classes three times a week for the next few weeks, and if you're smart, you'll show up for all the classes."

Tim moved over to join the others, and then everyone looked at Max.

"Thanks," Max said. "First, let me say I'm going to cover some basics that may help you, but if you get a chance to take a course through the local police department, I would encourage you to do that, too. The more you know, the safer you are."

He glanced around the room. Everyone was listening intently. Good. He wanted them to retain this information. "Let's start with awareness. Your number one way to protect yourself is to be aware of your surroundings at all times. Who is near you? Where could someone hide? What is going on around you?"

He glanced around the room. "Everyone close your eyes."

With a few giggles, the group did as he said. "Someone tell me what's sitting on the bar."

The group groaned and moaned and offered several excuses as to why they had no idea what was on the bar.

Then Paige said, "Two glasses, a cloth, a bowl, and Tim's water bottle."

Max grinned. Smart lady. Looked like she's already mastered this awareness of her surroundings thing.

"Everyone open your eyes and tell me if Paige is right," he said, already knowing she'd nailed it exactly.

"Paige, were you cheating?" Tim teased. "Because how did you know that?"

Paige looked more than a little self-conscious, and Max was fairly certain she hadn't meant to admit she knew what was on the bar.

"I have a good memory," she said.

"I'll say," Krystal said with a laugh. "I can barely remember where I've parked, let alone notice things like that."

Max moved forward. "That's the point. You need to be more aware. Let's talk about parking lots since they're a very dangerous area. Awareness is vital when you're in a parking lot. For starters, always know where your car is. And always approach your car with your keys in your hand, ready to get in, your head up, and your stride confident. Don't wander in the parking lot with your head down while you dig around in your purse for your keys."

"What about us guys?" Emilio said.

"Same goes for you. Always look confident. You know where you're going, you know who is around you, and you aren't an easy victim."

"So what you're trying to do is to be the least attractive potential victim, right?" Emilio said. "That makes them go find someone else, doesn't it?"

"Oh, now I don't like that," Tim said, shaking his head. "I don't want them going off to hurt someone else."

"It doesn't work that way," Annie said. "Right, Max? You can only take care of yourself. You can't worry about what happens to other people."

"I don't want anything to happen to anyone." Tim looked at Max. "So what can I do to keep everyone safe?"

"Nothing," Max admitted. "But you'll find that if you are confident and make it clear you're aware of what's going on around you, then you've created an environment that isn't comfortable to the bad guy. With any luck, he'll leave the area."

"Or she will," Emilio said. "Not all bad guys are men."

Tim and the other men all agreed, and Max bit back a sigh. "Fine, with any luck, he or she will leave the area."

Once the group seemed happy again, Max walked them through several more pointers about being aware and prepared. They ran through several tests, where he asked the group to notice their surroundings.

Then they went out to the parking lot and discussed possible trouble spots—areas that were especially dark and isolated at night, areas where someone could easily hide. By the time he finished, he felt like he'd given everyone in general—and Paige in particular—a good overview of how to be safe in parking lots.

"This is so helpful," Krystal told him. "I really appreciate it, and I'll always know where my car is from now on."

"Good," Max said, glad he could help. "And make certain you always have your keys ready."

She nodded. "Got it."

Paige wandered over, her smile so bright Max couldn't help smiling back. "I appreciate you doing this. I know you only volunteered to teach me, but I thought everyone could use the information."

"No problem, and I agree. It's good for them to know."

She kept smiling at him, and he knew she was curious as to why he'd sprinted away from her apartment last night like he'd caught on fire. Hell, in a way he had. The desire he'd felt for her last night had burned him.

Just like it was doing now.

"It's very nice of you," she said, tipping her head a little. Her smile seemed even brighter than before.

She was flirting with him, Max realized with a start. Damn.

"Glad I can help," he said, then at a loss for what else to do, he turned and headed across the room to the bar. He could feel Paige watching him, wondering about him, but there wasn't a thing he could say to her. Wasn't a thing he could do. He certainly couldn't act on what he was feeling. Only a scum would do that. And he didn't want to encourage her, because, well, that would make him a scum, too.

So what he needed was to think of a way to cool what was happening between them. There had to be some technique he could use that would let him still be friends with Paige without either one of them having an almost overwhelming desire to get the other naked.

He glanced at Paige, who was talking to Krystal. She looked so amazingly beautiful Max realized he was kidding himself. No way was he going to be able to be around that woman and not desire her. He was too aware of her, too attuned to her.

Of all the rotten luck.

"DON'T YOU THINK Max is great?" Krystal asked. "I'm so glad he works here. I mean, I should have realized it was stupid of me not to have my keys in my hand when I walked to my car. And that thing he said about looking inside your car makes a lot of sense. Don't want to discover while you're driving that someone is hiding in your back seat."

Paige had to admit, Max had given them some great advice today. And she hadn't been kidding when she'd thanked him for doing this. She did appreciate it.

The only thing that bothered her was the way he was acting around her. Last night, he'd taken off from her apartment like a man with the devil after him. And today, just when she thought they were hitting it off, he'd walked away.

"You like Max, don't you?" Krystal asked. "He seems like the perfect guy."

Paige looked at Krystal and tried to decide if the other woman was fishing for information. She knew some of the employees had noticed the look that had passed between her and Max last night. Plus, everyone knew he'd given her a lift home after work. One look at the grin on Krystal's face convinced Paige her friend was definitely trying to matchmake.

"Max is nice," she said, hoping Krystal would take the hint and drop it. "But everyone who works here is nice."

The older woman just continued to grin. "The two of you should have a lot of fun working on the Midsummer's Night thing. Personally, I think you should come up with something sexy and funky. Maybe hula skirts and coconut bras." She let out a little squeal. "Oh, and body-painting booths. Those are always hot."

Paige frowned. She didn't like the sound of this a bit. "Body painting booths?"

Krystal nodded. "Yep. For the guys. And the girls. Oh, and maybe the guys can wear the coconut bras, too." She giggled. "I think that would be a hoot."

Up until now, Paige hadn't given a lot of thought to this festival thing. Sure, she knew it was something she and Max needed to do, but she'd figured it involved setting up a few tables, maybe booking a local band. Margaritas under the stars kind of thing.

Nothing involving coconut bras and body painting.

"That doesn't sound too...um, classy," she said.

Krystal laughed so loudly that half the café turned to look at her. "It's not about class, Paige. It's about fun."

"Nine times out of ten, the police have to come," Tim said, walking over to join them. "Every year we try to keep it from turning into a mess—"

"But thankfully, you never succeeded," Krystal added.

This now sounded like the last thing on earth Paige would ever want to do let alone be capable of doing.

"Tim, you've definitely got the wrong person. I can't, and I don't want to, plan something like..." She waved one hand. "That."

Tim gave her a quick hug. "Paige, Paige, Paige. No one is saying you have to get everyone arrested. I know that's not your style. Like I said before, you and Max will make this Midsummer's Night *Festival* different from the others. You can make it classy, if you want. Heck, classy will be—"

"Boring?" Krystal shook her head. "It's not going to be the same if it's boring."

Sure, one of the things that had made Key West the perfect place to hide was its relaxed atmosphere. People hadn't bothered her. Her fellow employees hadn't pried or snooped. People had accepted her for who she'd said she was.

But that casual atmosphere looked like it was going to bite her big time with this festival. There was no way she was doing this.

"I can't," she told Tim.

Again, he laughed. "Yes, you can, and you will, and it will be great. I already told you, you're not required to make it something the police will need to raid. You're also not required to have body painting booths or whipped cream thong contests—"

"Oooh," Krystal said. "Now *that* sounds interesting. Max, definitely talk Paige into doing that."

Max had been drying the bar, but now he looked up. "Into doing what?"

Tim laughed. "You're going to hate this even more than Paige hates this."

"Whipped cream thongs," Krystal told Max, using her hands to draw what Paige assumed was a picture in the air. "I think you and Paige should look into things like that for the festival. Something...yummy."

"You're kidding, right?" Max scowled. "I'm not doing something like that."

Paige nodded. "That makes two of us."

Krystal sighed so loudly she sounded like a balloon deflating. "This is going to be the most boring festival in the history of the Sunset Café, Tim. You really should reconsider having these two plan it. No offense, Paige and Max, but you're like a couple of old coots. You need to loosen up if you're going to live here."

With that pronouncement, she walked away, muttering about boring people who had no sense of adventure. Paige looked at Max, who only shrugged.

"Now before you both start agreeing with Krystal, I want to reiterate that I have complete faith in you," Tim said, grinning broadly. "Food or foodlike substances of any sort are not required to make this festival a hit. I want you to bring your own sprit to the occasion. You're both new to the Keys. If you want to build a life here, you need to find your own rhythm. *Everyone* who wants to find a place to belong can find that place here." He leaned forward and tapped Paige on the nose. "Everyone, Paige. Regardless of what brings them here."

Tim walked away, leaving her staring after him. Although he didn't say anything specific, Paige knew he was suspicious of what had brought her here. Up until recently, he'd never mentioned her lack of references or the fact that she kept to herself in a place where everyone was very friendly with each other.

But during the last week or so, he seemed determined to draw her out, to get her more involved. As much as she wished she could truly join in here, she needed to keep a low profile.

This festival was the last thing a woman in hiding needed.

"Things keep getting stranger and stranger," Max said, leaning against the counter.

Paige looked at him and couldn't help wondering why he'd agreed to do this. Surely he had good references. Why didn't he just tell Tim to take a flying leap?

Paige continued to look at Max, who cocked an eyebrow at her. "What?" he finally asked.

"Why don't you tell Tim no?" she asked.

"Why don't you?" he countered.

"Because I'm a pushover," she said, grasping at the first excuse she could think of.

"Yeah, me, too," he said. Then he made a goofy face.

Laughter burst out of Paige. She'd laughed more in the last few days than she had in the last six months. Because of Max.

She'd found herself calming down since he'd arrived. In fact, she'd been thinking of a better way to deal with her problem. Running hadn't bought her anything but time. Sooner or later, she was going to have to face Brad and take control over her life. She just needed to develop a plan.

For the rest of the night, she thought of what she could do about Brad—that was when she wasn't thinking about Max. No matter how many times she told herself to end this preoccupation she had with the sexy bartender, she couldn't seem to stop herself from listening for his voice, smiling when he laughed.

She knew he wasn't trying to flirt with her. In fact, he seemed determined not to, but no matter how rational she tried to be, every time he grinned, she felt her heart beat faster. And when he looked directly at her, she felt her breath catch.

By the end of the night, she was so incredibly aware of the attraction she felt to Max that she could hardly carry her tray without dropping it. Glancing at the clock, she realized it was almost closing time and getting slow. She welcomed the chance to head into the storeroom to get some supplies.

Once inside, she leaned back against the shelves, closed her eyes, and willed her pulse to slow.

"You're being an idiot," she muttered.

"About what?"

Paige yelped and spun around. Max stood in the doorway. Figured. "What are you doing here?"

"I need napkins." He moved forward. "Why do you think you're an idiot?"

"Pick any of a million reasons," she said, trying to shift around him. The last thing she wanted was to be in such a tiny room with Max. She was having a terrible time controlling her emotions as it was.

"I need to get back to work," she murmured, trying to move past him.

Max blocked her way. "Hold on. Are you okay?"

The kindness in his voice really got to her. "Um, I'm fine." Insane, of course. But fine. She went to move past him again, but he stopped her once more.

"Paige, if something's bothering you, maybe I can help," he said, his deep voice washing over her.

"I'm fine," she repeated, hating how breathless her voice sounded.

"If you'd like to talk, just let me know," he offered, his voice sounding a little gruff.

"Thanks."

Feeling like the total idiot she'd already called herself, she spun around and headed toward the door.

Unfortunately she bumped straight into a tower of boxes instead.

After that, she wasn't sure exactly what happened in what order. She did know that at some point, the boxes tumbled and then she started to fall. And Max grabbed her to keep her from ending up on the floor.

But none of that surprised her.

What did surprise her was that somehow, she ended up kissing Max.

5

THE SECOND PAIGE'S LIPS touched his, Max knew he was in deep trouble. He had no idea how they'd ended up kissing, but man, was he glad they were. Without hesitation, he gathered her close and deepened the kiss. If he were honest, he'd wanted to kiss Paige ever since he'd met her.

Hell, he wanted to do a lot more than simply kiss her. Just the thought of being with her made need coil deep within him. He was a man who prided himself on his control, but control of any sort was out of the question at the moment.

Instead he backed Paige against one of the stacks of boxes and took over the kiss, slowing it. He wanted to take his time, to really savor this.

Not that she wasn't participating one hundred percent. She wrapped herself around him, tipped her head and teased his lips with her tongue. He'd give her this, the lady sure knew how to kiss.

When he opened his mouth to grant her access, she made a little mewing sound of pleasure. Max pulled her closer, molding her against him. He liked the way she felt, liked the way she smelled.

And man-o-man, he liked the way she kissed. Paige

put her whole body into kissing. Her lips were soft and seductive and Max was positive if he died at this moment, he'd have absolutely no regrets.

Max had no idea how long he stood there kissing Paige. One long, languid kiss followed another. First he'd take the lead, then she would. They both kept coming back for more, endlessly hungry for the taste of each other.

Periodically, common sense tried to scream at him to stop, but he ignored the voice and kept kissing Paige. As the minutes ticked by, though, that annoying voice kept getting louder and louder until finally it almost deafened him.

"Ah, hell," he muttered as he pulled his lips free from Paige's. She looked up at him, her eyes filled with desire, her lips puffy and pink from his kisses.

"Wow," she said, her voice little more than a whisper. "Thanks."

Thanks? She was thanking him for the kiss? He dropped his hands from her oh-so-tempting body and took a step back.

"We shouldn't have done that," he found himself saying even though he really didn't mean it. He'd enjoyed the kiss—a lot.

Rather than being upset, she smiled. "Well, I liked it."

"Yeah, well, I liked it, too. But we work together, Paige. We shouldn't get involved. Things could get complicated."

"Complicated how?"

Max scanned his brain, struggling to find the best way to get her to understand. He was still floundering when the door to the storage area opened. Tim stood in the doorway, one hand over his eyes. Max shook his head when he noticed the man's fingers were spread so he could see what was going on.

"I don't want to know what you two have been doing in here for so long, although I hope it was something amazing." He held out his other hand. "Just give me those napkins, okay? We're completely out and I can't wait any longer."

Max turned slightly so he blocked Paige from Tim's view. Then he grabbed a package of napkins and handed them to the other man.

"I'll be right out," he muttered.

Tim laughed. "Oh, don't rush. Take your time. Do what you need to do." He hollered over his shoulder. "Emilio, you should see what I'm not seeing."

When Max made an almost growling noise, Tim laughed again and then shut the door. "Have fun," he hollered through the thick wood.

Paige looked at Max. "I take it this is what you meant by complicated?"

No, it hadn't been, but he grabbed on to the excuse with both hands. "Yeah, we shouldn't do this. We work together. Complicated, like I said."

Paige nodded, but she still looked much too happy for Max's peace of mind. "I completely understand. We'll avoid complications."

She opened the door and flashed him another smile. "Oh, and thanks, again."

Then she walked out. Max stared after her, trying to figure out what had just happened. Trying to figure out how a man who prided himself on his self-control had completely lost it.

And trying to decide why Paige kept thanking him for making the worst mistake of his life.

PAIGE COULDN'T HELP smiling. Nothing could destroy the happiness she felt. Not Tim's lectures when he insisted it was his turn to drive her home that night, thereby robbing her of a chance to be alone with Max. Not even finding Diane sitting in front of her apartment looking sad and depressed could burst Paige's happiness bubble. She was too happy to be sad.

"Kyle found a house," Diane said glumly. "It has three bedrooms and two baths."

Paige unlocked her door and shut off the alarm. "Come on in and you can tell me all about it."

Diane finally dragged herself inside and flopped on the couch. Paige wanted to feel bad for her, but it was hard to sympathize. Kyle was a nice guy who adored Diane. Paige knew he wanted to build a life with her friend.

She'd love to have someone adore her the way Kyle did Diane.

That thought immediately conjured up an image of Max, and Paige ended up smiling again. The kiss had been amazing. No, better than amazing, it had been spectacular. She'd never been kissed like that before, and boy, she could hardly wait to kiss him again.

Complications or no complications, she knew one thing for certain, she and Max were far from done talking about this.

"The house is white. It has a yard and flowers." Diane groaned. "And a garage. Kyle said it's perfect for a minivan."

With that, Diane broke into loud, hiccuping sobs. Paige hurried over to her friend.

"It's okay, Diane. You simply need to tell Kyle how you feel. Explain that you're not ready for a house and a minivan."

Diane continued to sob, although Paige noticed she didn't seem to have any real tears. Her friend was nothing if not theatrical.

"He really wants this. He says it's time we move our relationship to the next phase. But I like the phase we're in now."

Paige patted Diane's hand. "He loves you. He wants to make a life with you."

Diane gasped, then she looked at Paige.

"You know what's next, don't you?"

Paige shook her head. "No. What's next?"

"Marriage," Diane wailed. "He's going to want to get married."

Maybe if she hadn't just been kissed to the point where she was weak at the knees, Paige would have understood Diane's concerns. But at the moment, having a great guy wanting to marry her didn't seem like such a terrible thing to Paige. Her only regret was that her life was so confused right now that she didn't know if getting involved with Max was fair to him.

She was going to have to give this some thought. As much as she might want to see where things went with Max, her life right now made that impossible. It wouldn't be fair to him to lead him on.

Diane had started sobbing again, so Paige patted her hand once more. "You've lived with Kyle for five years. It's like you're almost married now."

"But marriage is different. When you're married, you can't simply walk when things get uncomfortable."

"If you were going to walk out the first time things got uncomfortable, you would have left a long time ago," Paige pointed out. "You must love him."

"Of course I love him," Diane said, wiping her hands across her face even though there were no tears. "Loving him isn't the point."

"In that case, what does he say when you tell him you don't want a house and a minivan?"

Diane shrugged and looked away.

"You haven't told him, have you?" Paige asked, already knowing the answer to her question.

"He'll get upset," Diane said. "And then he'll probably break up with me."

"Of course he won't. He loves you."

Diane looked heartbroken. "I think he does, but what if this is more important to him?"

Rather than dismissing her concern, Paige gave it serious thought. She certainly wasn't an expert on relationships by any means. After all, there was a good chance the last man she'd loved was hunting her. But still, just because she'd never been lucky enough to be in love with someone great like Diane was didn't mean she was clueless as to how that love should work.

"If it's that important to him, then you should want to find a compromise if you truly love him," Paige finally said, certain her advice was correct.

"I guess. I mean I do want him to be happy. But what about my art? That's important to me, too, and I can't create in an environment like that."

"How do you know?" Paige reasoned. "You haven't even tried. You're simply giving up."

As she said the words, Paige realized she was doing the same thing. She was immediately assuming she couldn't see where things went with Max because of the way her life was right now.

But was that necessarily true or was she simply giving up?

"What if I move and can't create?" Diane asked.

"What if you move and can create so much more than you can now?" Paige warmed to her topic. "You can use one of those bedrooms as a studio. You've always wanted to paint landscapes. This is your chance."

Diane's expression brightened a little. "I could use a studio. Right now all of my things are smushed into that corner of the living room. It would be nice to have space."

"It would, wouldn't it?" Paige grinned. "I bet Kyle

was thinking along those lines. I bet he intended all along to make one of the rooms a studio for you."

"He does keep telling me the small bedroom has a great view and wonderful light."

"See? He's thinking of you."

She smiled. "I'm a nut, aren't I?"

"Yes. You are," Paige teased. "But that's what I like about you, and what Kyle loves about you."

"I guess I have to be open to new experiences," Diane said. "And explore all my options." She giggled. "Quick, what's another cliché I can use?"

"Love makes all things possible?" Paige offered.

Diane bobbed her head. "Good one. Okay, I'll go talk this over with Kyle."

"That's the best idea."

Diane unwound herself from the couch, then hugged Paige. "Thanks for listening to me. And don't forget, we still need to find a good mango for you."

Paige laughed. "I'm fine, thanks, though."

Diane was heading for the door, but she stopped and looked at Paige. "After I talk things through with Kyle, I'll ask him if he knows anyone for you. I bet he does."

"Don't," Paige told her friend, but the other woman kept walking out the door so she knew Diane hadn't listened to her.

It didn't matter anyway, because she had no intention of letting Diane and Kyle set her up.

If she wanted to get involved with someone, she already knew who she'd pick—now all she had to decide was should she.

MAX GLANCED ACROSS the car at Paige. It had been two days since their kiss and she was acting weird. Very weird. All night at work, she'd kept smiling at him and laughing at everything he said. He had a bad feeling about this. Whatever was making Paige act this way couldn't be good—not for an investigator trying to do his job.

And certainly not for a man trying to keep his hands to himself.

"Thanks again for the ride home," Paige said. The slightly breathy hitch to her voice made Max frown.

"No problem. I wanted to talk to you, anyway." He cleared his throat, trying to think of yet another way to say what he'd said before—the kiss notwithstanding, they couldn't get involved.

Paige laughed. "You sound so serious."

He frowned even more. "I am serious, Paige. I know we kind of—" He cleared his throat again. "I mean I know we had a great kiss, but that's all it was. One kiss. It didn't mean anything."

"I know. I wasn't expecting a declaration of love."

That was good. "Oh. Good."

"I have a lot going on in my life right now, and even though I'm attracted to you, now isn't the best time for me to get involved with someone."

He couldn't agree more. "Yeah. Me, too."

"You, too, what?" she asked.

He hadn't thought that far ahead. He scrambled for an explanation. "I just moved to town, started a new job. I'm not looking to get involved now."

He glanced over at Paige. Good. They agreed on this. That was a relief.

"I completely understand," she said. And for a few minutes, neither of them said a word. When she did finally speak, all she said was, "The kiss was great, though."

Man, he'd been hoping not to talk about it. "Yeah. Great. But wrong."

"Hmm." She was looking out the window, and that soft murmur of agreement she'd made didn't do a thing to calm his nerves. She was thinking about the kiss. Reliving it. He knew it. And the longer she sat there saying nothing, the more the kiss played back in his mind, too.

Yeah, it had been a good one. A really good one.

"Whoa, don't forget to turn here," she said, interrupting his thoughts. "My apartment is down this street, remember?"

Max made the turn without really thinking. Man, he needed to get a grip. Forcing all thought of the kiss out of his unruly mind, he said, "I'll get your car fixed tomorrow."

"I can get it fixed myself," she said. "You've already done enough for me."

"I don't know, Paige. I'm still struggling with those Neanderthal impulses," he teased, trying to change the mood in the car. "Maybe you should let me do this one last macho thing."

She laughed. "Now how will that help? If you do

this, it will only reinforce that macho side of your personality."

The lady had a point. "Okay, how about we compromise and we do it together. I can meet you here first thing in the morning and we'll handle your car together. That way, I'll still be helping without doing it myself. This could end up being a major step in my psychological development."

Paige laughed again. "Fine. If you truly feel you need this so your psyche doesn't suffer—"

"And I do."

"Then far be it from me to deny you."

Max pulled into her apartment's parking lot and found a spot. "Thanks. You're a real friend."

He parked the car, then without asking, climbed out. He knew they still had to watch for Collier. He couldn't forget his reason for being here.

He headed over to the other side of the car, intending to open the door for Paige, but she'd already climbed out. She made no comment as she headed toward the stairs. Looked like the whole kiss subject was behind them.

As they walked, Max once again found himself admiring the gentle sway to Paige's hips as she climbed the stairs in front of him. He tried to look away. Tried to think about something else. Tried not to let it turn him on.

But it didn't work. He couldn't help imagining sliding his hands around her hips and pulling her close. He'd snuggle that cute little bottom of hers against him, then he'd lean down and nibble on her oh-so-sexy neck.

Slowly he'd slide his hands across her flat stomach, his fingers flexing against her flesh. Then, once she was breathing heavily, he'd lower one hand, inch by sweet inch, until he was caressing her—

"Apartment."

Max felt like he'd slammed into a brick wall. He shook his head, trying to get out the image that had lodged there. He realized Paige was staring at him, a puzzled looked on her face.

"My apartment. We're at my apartment," she said, obviously not for the first time.

With effort, Max pulled himself together. What was wrong with him? He had to stop having sex fantasies about this woman.

He glanced over her shoulder. Sure enough. They were standing directly outside her apartment.

"Let me open the door for you," he said. She probably thought that was his way of inviting himself inside, but it was actually his way of checking out her place.

She handed him the keys. "My self-defense instructor told me to always have my keys ready, so I took them out of my purse before we got out of the car."

Max looked at her huge purse. "How'd you ever find them in there?"

Paige lifted the bag. "I have a compartment I put them in so I can find them quickly."

"I don't own enough stuff to fill that purse," he said dryly.

Again she laughed. "I subscribe to the be-prepared philosophy. I have makeup, tools, my wallet, CDs." She pulled out a canister. "Pepper spray."

Max took a half step back. "Keep it away from me. That stuff is evil."

"That's the point," she said. "I want to be able to defend myself."

"Let me run you through some guidelines on using that stuff," he said. "I want to make certain you don't wind up on the receiving end."

"Okay." She nodded toward the door. "You going to unlock it or kick it in as a display of your macho prowess?"

Max chuckled and dangled the key chain. "I think I'll try the civilized approach just to be different."

He studied her key chain. He'd barely noticed it the other night, but it was huge. She had all sorts of things hanging off it. A plastic four-leaf clover. A small silver horseshoe. A tiny wishing well.

"Think you've got enough things on this?" he teased. Then added, "You could use this as a weapon. Hit an attacker in the face with this, and it will knock him out for a couple of hours."

Paige groaned. "Very funny. It's my lucky charm. Whenever I come across something that claims to be lucky, I add it to my key chain."

He raised one eyebrow and studied her pretty face in the bright light from the lamp by her door. He felt something tug at him, some emotion he didn't want to think about, didn't want to even consider.

But it was there, and it unnerved him. He cleared his throat and focused on the key chain in his hand. "So has this brought you luck?"

"Not yet," she admitted with a self-conscious laugh. "But I keep hoping one day I'll find the right charm, and then my luck will change."

Although he knew why good luck was so important to Paige, he pretended to be curious. "What's so terrible about your luck? Seems to me you're doing okay."

He watched as she debated what to say. He surprised himself by hoping she'd tell him the truth. Not that she should. That wouldn't be smart. And even though he knew Paige had come to trust him, she shouldn't tell him a thing.

When she did finally answer, she played it smart. "Doesn't everyone wish they had good luck?" was all she said. Then she pointed to one of the many keys hanging from the key chain. "That one opens the front door."

Inwardly Max congratulated her on being a wise woman. Paige had done the right thing. No matter how much she thought she knew about him, the bottom line was she was fighting for her life. She couldn't afford to make stupid mistakes.

As he opened the front door, Max told himself to remember that very same rule. He couldn't afford any stupid mistakes, either.

So he had to find a way to keep himself focused. To keep his mind off how much he wanted to touch her, how much he wanted to kiss her again.

"Do you want to come inside?" She smiled softly. "I promise I won't attack you with my pepper spray."

That was the least of his worries. The job required him to take care of her, and this was the perfect opportunity to go inside and check things out. His fear was his libido would be too interested in checking out other things than just her apartment.

Realizing she was waiting for his answer, he steeled his resolve and said, "Okay. Sure." Then he added more for his own benefit than for hers, "But only for a couple of minutes."

He led the way inside and looked around. He didn't want to make her suspicious, but he did want to make certain her apartment was safe.

"Where's your dog?" he asked, suddenly on alert when he didn't hear the familiar barking.

"I knew I was going to be late tonight so I asked my neighbor to watch Sugar."

A light pink flush tinted her face, and Max frowned. Did she mean what he thought she meant? Surely she didn't think he'd make love to her just because they'd kissed?

"Want something to drink?" She smiled a sexy little smile.

"Paige, I thought you understood that the kiss was a mistake," he said.

She walked by him to the kitchen. "Calm down, I'm not going to jump you. We're friends. I'm just being friendly."

He wasn't too sure about that. Her tone sounded

normal and casual, but that smile. That smile meant trouble.

He needed to get out of here before something bad happened.

"I probably should head on home," he said.

Paige didn't seem the least upset by his announcement. "You could stick around for a while, and we could go over some ideas for the festival."

Max ran a tired hand across his face. "I'd forgotten about that."

"Tim and Emilio haven't," she said. "Every time I'm anywhere near one of them, he grabs me and asks me how it's coming. I've been thinking about it, and I feel we should do something different."

Max glanced at the front door. So close yet so far away. "Different from their usual debauchery? Sounds good to me."

Paige laughed, the sound light and free. "Yes. I'm not interested in doing anything they suggested."

She ran across the room and picked up a notebook. Obviously she'd given this some thought. Max felt guilty about that. He'd forgotten all about this stupid festival.

Walking toward him, Paige flipped open the notebook. "I've been thinking—this festival is about Key West, right? About living in the Keys and being part of Key West."

"I guess."

"So what better way to make it about living in Key West than get the local charities involved?"

She said this with a flourish, and Max chuckled.

"I'm lost," he admitted. "The way Tim and Emilio explained it, the festival sounds like a get drunk and party kind of thing."

"That's in the past." She flipped to a page in the middle of the notebook, then set it on the table in the hall. "See, this is what I have in mind. All the local charities I've called so far are interested. They should pick up some donations, we should draw a big crowd for the Sunset, and everyone should be happy."

Max glanced at the diagram she'd carefully drawn in her notebook. Paige was putting together some sort of carnival or arcade thing where the charities had games for people to play. He reached out and flipped through the notebook. There were pages and pages of drawings and research. She'd put a ton of work into this.

"Wow. You've really worked hard," he said. "I think it sounds great."

She flashed a dazzling smile at him, and Max felt like he'd taken a hit to the solar plexus. Paige made him feel things he'd never felt before, never thought he'd feel.

He cleared his throat and looked away. "Bet Tim and Emilio will be surprised."

"Let's not tell them. They may want to change it, and I'm not interested in doing the kind of festival they've had before."

"Sounds smart." Max shut the book and turned to face you. "How can I help?"

"I need some more charities called, and I'll need help putting together the booths."

"Okay." He looked longingly at the front door again. He needed to get out of here now. "You've done a great job, Paige. You should be proud of yourself."

"You know something, I am," she said with a self-conscious laugh. "I've been caught up with my own problems for a long time, and it felt good to focus on something else."

He'd bet it had. "You did great," he told her again.

For a second, she just looked at him, her gaze sweet and soft. Max told himself to walk away, to head for the door right now, but his damn feet seemed glued to the floor.

"You're a nice man," she said. "I'm glad you're my friend."

Her friend? He blew out a breath of self-disgust. A friend wouldn't be lying to her. A friend wouldn't be lusting after her.

So no, he didn't think he was her friend.

Man, he needed to get out of here. "I'll be back in the morning to help with the car."

She must have sensed his mood, because she nodded and led the way to the front door. "Okay. But you really don't have to help with my car. I'm a grown woman who is perfectly capable of taking care of herself."

"I know. But I want to do this." He couldn't really explain why it was important to him to help. Part of it was because it made it easier to keep an eye on her, but that was a small part of it. Mostly he wanted to be with her. He liked being around Paige.

He liked it too much.

"Well, I guess I'll see you in the morning," he said, trying to ignore the desire humming between them.

"I guess you will." She walked over to stand next to him and smiled.

"Have a good night," he said, wondering why he hadn't left yet.

"You, too." Her smile grew even larger.

It took some effort, but Max finally got one foot to move forward. Steeling his resolve, he moved the other foot, too. "Thanks."

Then he made a fatal mistake and looked at her again. That same emotion he'd felt earlier rushed through him. Paige made him feel so much more than simple lust. Lust he could handle. Lust he could walk away from.

But this closeness, this emotional tug he felt whenever he looked into her clear green eyes, made it impossible to leave.

So he didn't. He stood there, looking at her beautiful face. Man, he wanted to kiss her. Just one kiss. One short kiss would be enough.

With effort, he reached for the doorknob. "Night."

As soon as he opened the door, he went to walk by her, and then she did it. He hadn't even seen it coming, hadn't had even a second's warning before Paige reached out and gave him a hug.

"I really am glad you're my friend," she said.

It was a quick hug, nothing romantic or sexual, but she might as well have set him on fire, because that was all it took to make his self-control dry up faster than a grape in the sun.

Before she could pull away or say anything else, those feelings that had been gathering inside him broke free. Without hesitation, he buried his hands in her hair and gathered her close.

Then he kissed her.

6

PAIGE HADN'T expected him to kiss her. Sure, she'd hoped he might, even though it wasn't sensible. She'd accepted that they weren't going to act on the attraction they felt for each other.

But the second Max kissed her, she was glad he'd given into what they both were feeling. When he deepened the kiss, she willingly let him coax her lips apart and dip his tongue inside. His chest rumbled with a satisfied growl as she met his ardor with her own. She slipped her arms around his neck, her fingers threading through the hair on the back of his head, sculpting him to her. Rising on her toes, she burned her body against his, her mouth closing around his tongue and keeping it prisoner.

One kiss followed another until they both were both breathless with desire.

"We shouldn't be doing this," Max murmured, as he trailed kisses down her neck. "Like you said, we shouldn't get involved."

His words might have had more impact on her if he hadn't said them in a voice rough with passion.

"Maybe I was wrong about that getting involved thing," she said, leaning up and dropping another kiss on his lips. She took her time kissing him, letting herself savor the sensation. "Hmmm. Yes. I definitely was wrong about that not getting involved thing."

He leaned away from her, his gaze serious. "No, you were right. Neither of us can get involved in anything long-term right now."

Paige couldn't dispute that. She had no idea if she'd even be in Key West a month from now. Heck, she didn't know if she'd be here a week from now, although she certainly hoped so.

Her gaze landed on his lips and desire tingled through her. She'd never wanted a man the way she wanted Max at this moment. Never felt this alive before.

When Max started to remove his hands from her waist, the sense of loss hit Paige hard. She didn't want this to end.

"Um, I don't suppose you'd consider something short-term," she blurted.

Max froze. "What?"

The more she thought about this, the more she liked the idea. "Who says this has to be long-term? We can have something short-term. What's wrong with that?"

She was hoping Max would like the idea as much as she did, but instead, he frowned. "Paige, I don't think that's a good idea."

She sensed he was trying to be noble. He probably thought she'd get hurt because she'd end up falling for him. But that wouldn't happen because she wouldn't fall in love with anyone at the moment. Not until this thing with Brad was settled.

But Max didn't know that, so she tried to explain the best she could. "I'm sorry I can't get involved right now, but I do think we could have some fun. If we both agree that's all it is, I don't see what harm there is."

Max took a step back from her. She was glad to see that rather than frowning, he now looked uncertain. Uncertain was good. It meant he was starting to change his mind.

"I don't know," he said, but his gaze was on her lips and she could see the fire of desire burning hot in his eyes. "There are a lot of things you don't know about me."

True. But the last few months had taught her to trust her instincts, and her instincts told her Max was a good guy.

Still, to humor him, she asked, "Ever killed anyone?"

He frowned. "No. But—"

"Hit a woman?"

"Of course not."

"Are you married?"

"No. Paige, listen I still—"

"Committed a felony?"

"No."

"Do you like dogs?"

He blinked. "What?"

"Dogs. Do you like dogs? Sugar is very important to

me, and I could never hang around with someone who didn't like my dog."

He chuckled. "Yeah, I like dogs."

She smiled. "Good. Then that's all I need to know right now. And for the record, there are many, many things you don't know about me." She held up one hand and ticked off her items. "Just so you know, though, I've never killed someone or hit a man or a woman, I'm not married, I've never committed a felony, and I love dogs."

He sighed. "Paige, I still don't think you're the short-term kind. This could be a disaster."

"True. But only if we make it into one. I know, let's set some ground rules to guarantee that nothing goes wrong," she said, reaching out and lightly rubbing his chest. She liked touching Max. Liked it a lot. But then again, she liked everything about Max. The way he smiled. The way he made her laugh. The sweet way he worried about her.

Oh, and the way he kissed her so her knees buckled.

She drew little circles on his T-shirt, flexing her fingers once or twice against his muscles. When he made no move to stop her, she felt like doing a happy dance.

"I think rules are a good idea," she said absently.

"Rules? Like what?" His voice was raspy and deep, but she didn't miss that she'd caught his interest.

Paige considered the question for a second, and then said, "No taking this too seriously."

"That's it? One rule?"

"It's a big rule," she teased, leaning up and kissing

his jaw. "It's the only rule we need when you think about it."

When she flicked her tongue against his skin, he groaned like a man in pain.

"I shouldn't do this," he said.

Paige leaned back and looked at him. "Do you want to?"

He looked like a man hanging on to his last shred of self-control. "You know I do. But I don't want to hurt you."

Although she appreciated the thought, she hurried to assure him, "Then there's nothing to worry about because I want this. You're not going to hurt me. I'm not going to hurt you. It's the rule." She thought for a moment, then teased, "Would it help if I swear on your brother's head?"

He chuckled and pulled her close. "I can't fight both of us."

"Good. Then don't fight either of us," she said, thrilled he'd agreed. She'd never acted this way before, but there was something about Max that made her feel and do things she'd never considered possible. He was more than just a man she desired. He was a man she liked and admired. A man she was happy to have in her life. "My bedroom's down the hall."

He hesitated for a second, and she was afraid he was going to change his mind. So to distract him, she kissed his neck, her mouth gliding over his skin, her tongue trailing moisture on his flesh. When he still didn't make a move, she tugged his shirt free of his jeans.

"You're thinking again. I thought you macho Neanderthals didn't do that."

He chuckled, but the sound became more of a groan when she slipped one hand under his T-shirt and rested it on his warm, bare chest. "I'm pretty sure my brain isn't working at all right now."

"All your blood leaving your brain, is it?" she teased. "Good. That's the way I like my men—"

"Dumb?"

"Sexy and distracted," she corrected.

"Ah. Well, before I get too distracted, where did you say that bedroom was?" Without waiting for her answer, he picked her up in his arms. Paige squeaked with surprise, then settled against his chest. This was nice. He was within easy kissing distance this way.

Never a lady to miss an opportunity, she took full advantage of having him so close. She kissed him deeply, exploring his mouth with her tongue.

For a second, Max kissed her back. Then he broke the contact and headed down the hall to her bedroom. She tried to kiss him again, but he wouldn't let her.

"That lack of blood problem," he told her. "I can only do one thing at a time."

She giggled. "Then let me think about what I want that one thing to be."

When they reached her room, he set her on the ground. In the past, Paige had always felt shy with a new lover, but not with Max. She felt comfortable with him. A large part of that had to do with the way he looked at her, like she was the most beautiful woman he'd ever seen.

She tugged at his T-shirt, and he pulled it over his head. "You're in a hurry."

"I feel like I've been waiting for this my whole life," she admitted.

Max turned and looked at her. "Yeah. Me, too."

Paige smiled. Good. She was glad he felt what she was feeling. Reaching out, she ran one hand across his bare chest. "Nice chest."

He nodded at her T-shirt. "Wish I could say the same thing."

She laughed, surprised at how much fun she was having. "Is that some sort of veiled hint?"

"I didn't think there was a thing veiled about it," he said, leaning down and kissing her. He nudged her toward the bed. "I think I need to lie down. That blood problem again."

She crawled on the bed and pulled him down next to her. "You poor Neanderthal."

"It's sad, isn't it?" He reached out and pulled her T-shirt free of her shorts. "What will we do to help me?"

Smiling, Paige pulled her T-shirt over her head. "Well, does that help?"

He made a groaning, gurgling noise when he saw her peach-colored lace bra. "Trust me, I have even less blood in my brain now than I did before."

She pretended to be surprised. "Really?" With a flick

of her fingers, she popped open the bra's clasp and pulled the fragile garment off. "How about now?"

Max cupped her breasts gently, his thumbs circling her taut nipples. "I have absolutely no blood left in my brain at all," he murmured right before he leaned over and took one nipple in his mouth.

That made two of them, because as soon as his lips touched her, Paige lost the ability to think about anything except this man. Pleasure washed over Paige, and she ran her fingers through his hair, holding him to her. When he shifted his attention to her other breast, she closed her eyes, letting the sensations roll across her.

"You taste sweet," he said, kissing his way back to her mouth. "Like heaven."

She liked that. In fact, she liked everything about Max. As they kissed, she skimmed one hand down his chest and fiddled with the top button of his jeans, finally popping it free. He kept kissing her as he did the same. They both slid zippers down at the same time. Then he broke the kiss, winked at her, and shucked off his jeans and boxers in record time.

Paige followed his lead, slipping off her shorts and panties, then sliding up against him. For a long moment, they simply looked at each other, their gazes tangled just like their bodies were. She felt his heart beating and knew he felt hers, too.

Feelings Paige hadn't expected filled her. Feelings of rightness. Of belonging. Of being secure.

She smiled at Max, who smiled sweetly back at her. He was feeling it, too. She could tell.

He leaned forward and gave her a gentle, loving kiss. When he ended the kiss, Paige reached over into the nightstand drawer and pulled out a condom.

"Better get a few," he said.

She shot him a teasing look. "Really? Feeling energetic?"

"Definitely." He took the condom and quickly slipped it on. As soon as he was done, she climbed on top of him, sliding onto his length.

"Wow," she said, settling firmly on top of him.

"Exacting what I was thinking." He reached up and plucked at her tight nipples.

Paige closed her eyes and let the sensations roll over her. Then she started to move. Slowly at first, then faster and faster, chasing the ultimate pleasure she knew awaited her.

Max matched her rhythm, thrusting deep inside her, bringing her ever closer.

With each passing moment, Paige felt the tension inside her increase, spiraling upward until she could hardly breathe. She rode Max faster and faster until desire overwhelmed them both.

Then she held his gaze as release washed over them like a tidal wave.

MAX OPENED HIS EYES and drew in a deep breath. He felt terrific for all of ten seconds before guilt hit him like a sucker punch.

Damn. He'd made love to Paige. Not once. Not even twice. But several times during the course of a night that had consisted of lots of lovemaking and very little sleep.

What was wrong with him? Glancing over at her, he realized the question was rhetorical. Something about Paige got to him, and whatever it was, it caused him to do stupid things. Really stupid things. Normally that wouldn't bother him, but those stupid things could put Paige in danger.

As he watched her sleep, he felt desire flare within him again. Oh, no. Not this morning. This morning he was going to be smart, so he slipped out of bed and pulled on his jeans and shirt. He'd go give Travis a call. That would take his mind off of how tempting Paige looked all rumpled and sexy.

Walking softly, he headed out of her apartment and down the stairs. A young woman was outside walking two dogs, one of which was Sugar. The woman openly watched him come down the stairs and head toward his car.

Max knew this woman was a friend of Paige's. He'd seen her stop by to visit Paige many times during the couple of weeks he'd been watching the apartment. No doubt as soon as he drove off later this morning, this woman was going to be on Paige's doorstep demanding details.

This was going to make being on stakeout more difficult, if not impossible. Now not only Paige knew what his car looked like, but so did this woman.

"Good morning," the woman said, heading toward him like a heat-seeking missile. "I'm Diane Mitchell. And you are?"

Wow, talk about direct. Max leaned against his car. "Max Walker."

"What do you do for a living, Max?"

He bit back a smile. It was obvious this woman meant business. "I'm a bartender."

"Where Paige works?"

Sugar came over and sniffed Max's shoes, so he bent and patted the dog. "Yes. I work at the Sunset."

"How long have you been there?"

Max stood and smiled. "A few weeks. How long have you known Paige?"

Diane waved one hand. "We're talking about you. Intend on being anything other than a bartender?"

He chuckled, which only made Diane frown. "Sorry. I'll think about it. I just got out of the Navy, so I'm trying to figure out what I want to do."

"Kinda old to be figuring out what you want to be when you grow up," she said flatly.

"Better late than never."

"Why Key West?"

"Because it's a beautiful place."

"You graduate from high school?"

That one made him laugh, which only caused Diane's frown to deepen. "Yes, ma'am. I graduated from high school. I have some college, too."

"Some?"

"Two years." He glanced at his watch. As entertaining as this was, he wanted to call Travis and pick up breakfast for Paige. "It's been really nice meeting you."

Apparently his message wasn't as clear as he'd thought it was. "Got any family?" she asked.

"I have a brother." He flashed her his best smile. "Let me make this simple for you, Diane. I'm not married or engaged and I don't have any children. I've never committed a crime, don't have any tattoos, and don't smoke. I really like Paige. I have no intention of hurting her."

Sugar was jumping, so he scratched her behind the ears. "Hey, Sugar."

"You know Sugar?"

"Yep."

"I see."

She considered him for a couple of seconds, and finally said, "Treat Paige well."

Then without waiting for him to respond, she turned and walked away.

Max stared after her. Man, he'd have to emulate her the next time he had to question someone. Her machine-gun approach to information gathering was nothing if not effective.

Shaking his head, he climbed into his car and drove to the doughnut shop down the street. After getting some food, he dialed Travis's cell phone number.

"Where have you been? You should have checked in yesterday," Travis said the second he answered. "Is Paige okay? Did something happen?"

"Whoa. Everything is fine. Sorry I didn't call sooner,

but I've been busy," he said, pushing the thought of what he'd been busy doing out of his mind. "Everything okay there?"

"No, bro," Travis said. "Something's up. The agency has been getting weird phone calls. Lots of hang-ups. Lots of strange people calling. I figured something was wrong, so I decided to stay here last night and keep an eye on the place."

Max didn't like the sound of this one bit. "And?"

"And about 2:00 a.m., a couple of guys tried to break in. I flipped on the light and scared them off."

Dread settled over Max. "Did you get a look at them?"

"No. I was dozing in my desk chair, and the second I heard someone at the door, I hit the light. They took off before I even reached the door. By the time I got to the street, they were long gone."

Damn. Max didn't like the thought of Travis being there alone with that kind of trouble. His brother could have been hurt, or worse, killed. These people meant business.

"Next time, call the police," he told his brother. "No hero stuff."

"Gee, too bad I don't know a private investigator. You know, someone trained in security. Someone who's paid a lot of money to be a bodyguard." He laughed. "That would come in handy."

Max realized his brother was right, but he still didn't like the thought of Travis being in serious danger. His brother was new at this and often acted before thinking.

"You want to hear my theory?" Travis asked.

"That you were a jerk chasing after them since they could have been waiting for you," Max said flatly. "You have to use caution. Think the situation through before you act."

"Fine. I'll think it through next time. That should guarantee that they have plenty of time to get away."

Max groaned. "CYA, Trav."

"Works both ways. You'd better CYA, too, because I think those guys were after information on Paige. I think they were going to look for an address for her since the Atlanta one obviously was bogus," Travis said.

"You don't know for a fact this has to do with Paige," Max pointed out, even though he figured there was a good chance he was whistling past the grave-yard. "Maybe this is about a different case we're work-ing on. Paige isn't the only person we're working with."

"Come on. Get serious. You think this is about Mrs. Delaney wanting us to find her lost dog? Or how about TeleTech wanting us to beef up their alarm system? Or maybe Fred Johnson wanting us to find out if his wife is fooling around with the pool man?"

"Very funny." Max ran one hand across his fore-head. Travis was right. As much as he hated to admit it, there was only one case that would draw that kind of action.

Paige was in danger. Real danger. He glanced at his watch. He'd been gone almost a half-hour. He needed to get back to the apartment and stay close to her from now on.

Almost as if he'd read his mind, Travis said, "You have to stay glued to Paige, bro. I mean it. I've got a bad feeling about this. These guys might have taken off last night, but I know they haven't given up on finding her. That means that sooner or later, trouble is going to be heading your way."

"I've got it," he assured Travis.

Something in his voice must have made Travis suspicious. "Nothing's wrong, is it?"

"No," Max told him. "I know how to do my job."

"And I know how to do mine," Travis said. "Something's wrong. I can sense it. So tell me what's the problem. Do you need help?" He laughed, and then added, "Because I won't have a problem staying close to Paige. You can come back here and help Mrs. Delaney hunt down that lost dog of hers."

Max grunted, because in his opinion, that's all the response his brother deserved. Besides, he had other things on his mind. Make that he had another person on his mind. He'd already restarted his car and was driving back to Paige's apartment. He'd been away too long.

"I got to go. Call me on my cell if anything else happens," Max said, hanging up as he turned down the street that led to Paige's apartment.

He had to face facts. He had the perfect setup here.

As Paige's lover, he would be expected to hang around her all the time. She understood there were things about him she didn't know. She was okay with that. She'd made it clear last night she didn't care.

Still, he wasn't dumb enough to think she wasn't going to care once she found out who he was and why he was here.

But he couldn't worry about that now. He had to keep Paige safe. That was all that mattered.

HE'D BROUGHT HER DOUGHNUTS. Paige had just stepped out of the shower when she saw Max standing in the doorway to the bedroom swinging a bag of doughnuts in one hand.

"Sorry I wasn't here when you woke up this morning, but I thought you might need some food." The grin he flashed was downright devilish. "You know, to regain your strength."

Paige laughed and walked over to him. She took the bag from him and glanced inside. "Yum, chocolate covered doughnuts."

She took the bag and sat on the side of the bed. Pulling out a doughnut, she offered it to him. "Want one?"

"In a sec." Instead he leaned over and kissed her. Paige returned his kiss eagerly. She loved kissing Max. She always felt the impact clear to her toes.

When he ended the kiss, he winked and took a bite out of her doughnut. Paige laughed.

"Hey, no fair. Get your own."

"Yours tastes better," he said with a straight face.

"No, it doesn't."

He dipped one finger in the chocolate frosting, and then dabbled it across her bottom lip. As he licked the icing off her, he murmured, "Yeah, it tastes much, much better."

Paige caught her breath as he removed all the chocolate from her mouth. He did a very thorough job that made her squirm with desire by the time he was done.

"Definitely tasty," Max said once he was done.

Deciding two could play at this game, Paige took some frosting and pulled up his T-shirt. After spreading it along his chest, she pushed him flat on the bed and set to work. Max chuckled at first, but as she worked, his laughter turned into a groan of pleasure.

When she was finished, Paige sat next to him and grinned. "You're right. It tastes better this way."

He glanced down at the towel she'd wrapped around herself, then snagged the bag of doughnuts. Pulling out one covered in frosting, he gave her a sexy, devilish grin. "What should I do now?"

Paige went to scoot away from him, but she wasn't quick enough. She was giggling as he flicked open her towel.

"I'm very hungry," he said, dipping his index finger into the frosting.

"Hmmm, poor thing." Paige felt her heart race as he leaned closer. Paige felt her nipples tighten in anticipation, and held her breath as he slowly reached out and painted them with chocolate.

"Now *that's* what I call delicious," he said, carefully

The Harlequin Reader Service® — Here's how it works:

Accepting your 2 free books and mystery gift places you under no obligation to buy anything. You may keep the books and gift and return the shipping statement marked "cancel." If you do not cancel, about a month later we'll send you 4 additional books and bill you just $3.80 each in the U.S., or $4.47 each in Canada, plus 25¢ shipping & handling per book and applicable taxes if any.* That's the complete price and — compared to cover prices of $4.50 each in the U.S. and $5.25 each in Canada — it's quite a bargain! You may cancel at any time, but if you choose to continue, every month we'll send you 4 more books, which you may either purchase at the discount price or return to us and cancel your subscription.

*Terms and prices subject to change without notice. Sales tax applicable in N.Y. Canadian residents will be charged applicable provincial taxes and GST. Credit or Debit balances in a customer's account(s) may be offset by any other outstanding balance owed by or to the customer.

removing every speck of chocolate with his tongue whirling and whirling around her taut nipples.

Paige gasped as desire shot through her. "Max," she said, combing her hands through his hair as he took her nipple deep into his mouth.

While he suckled, his hands roved her body, skimming lightly over her skin, teasing her, tormenting her, tempting her into greater passion.

"You're very talented," she murmured and he slid one hand between her legs and caressed her.

Max chuckled softly, his breath warm against her breasts. "We Neanderthals have our moments."

With precision and care, he used his fingers and his palm to coax her closer and closer to release. He caressed her gently, never stopping the magical rhythm.

As passion pulled her deeper into its spell, he kissed her lips. Then her shoulders. Next her right breast, lingering for a moment before continuing on his journey. Paige felt the tension rising in her body. Release was so close. So very close.

Max dipped his tongue into her navel, making Paige squirm with pleasure. She shifted her legs, needing what only Max could give her. He replaced his hand with his mouth, his lips and tongue sending indescribable joy through her. She couldn't think, couldn't move, couldn't do anything but focus on the sensations he was creating.

The release she craved all too soon found her, and the waves of pleasure overtook her. The experience was so intense, so complete that when it was over, she remained still for quite some time, savoring the feeling.

When she finally opened her eyes, Max was calmly finishing the chocolate-covered doughnut. He grinned at her. "This is good."

Paige laughed and grabbed one of the doughnuts. Pushing him back on the bed, she said, "Yes. Very, very good."

7

"YOU LOOK LIKE a happy man," Tim observed when Max walked into the Sunset later that day. He narrowed his eyes, and then looked at Paige. "Hey, you look happy, too."

Max went to walk past the other man, but Tim stopped him. "Oh. My. God. You two have been consenting adults."

This wasn't good. The last thing he needed was for Tim to broadcast the news to the entire world.

"Don't go there," Max said firmly.

Not surprisingly, Tim didn't drop the subject. In fact, he seemed as delighted as a toddler on Christmas morning.

"This is fabulous." He gave Paige a hug, and when he looked like he might give Max one, too, Max growled. With a laugh, Tim backed up.

"Okay, I get it. No touching." He looked at Paige, then Max, and laughed again. "I knew this was going to happen."

Before either Max or Paige could say anything, Tim hollered, "Emilio, you won't believe who's involved."

He said it in a singsong voice that made Max groan.

"Drop it," he told Tim again, and just like before, the other man ignored him.

Emilio wandered out from the kitchen, looked at Max, then Paige, then laughed. "The salt worked. I told you it would."

"You were right," Tim said. "As always."

"Salt always works." Emilio grinned at Paige. "Congrats, sweetheart."

Then with a wave to Max, he disappeared back into the kitchen and promptly started to tell everyone very loudly about the new couple.

Max looked at Paige. She seemed partly amused, partly annoyed by Tim's and Emilio's reactions. He winked at her, which made her laugh.

"I have to get to work," Paige finally said.

"Me, too," Max said.

"What? No details?" Tim sighed.

"No details," Paige told him.

"No fair. And here I was all set to tell you about the phone call you received today even though you did absolutely nothing for me."

Max froze, his gaze immediately going to Paige. She seemed to pale before his eyes. Obviously she didn't get phone calls at work.

"What phone call?" she asked. Max could hear the anxiety in her voice, but obviously Tim didn't. He went on and on about the call coming in right in the middle of the lunch rush and how difficult it was to understand the man on the other end.

"I mean, cell phones are great, but you shouldn't call

other people unless you've got a strong signal. That's simple common courtesy. People should—"

Paige cut him off. "What did this man say? Did he give you his name?"

"Naw. In fact, he didn't even know your name. He just asked for, and I quote, 'the hot blond babe.'"

Paige was nibbling on her bottom lip. She was obviously scared, but if Max had to guess, he'd lay money on this guy being someone who'd stopped into the bar and now wanted to ask Paige out. He wanted to reassure Paige and tell her he didn't think this had anything to do with Brad, but he could hardly do that when as far as she was concerned, he knew nothing about what was happening.

"Did he say anything else?" Paige asked.

"No. And he sounded like he was about fifteen. He kept calling me dude." Tim shuddered. "I hate that. Makes me feel like I should be wearing tropical clothes and hanging out by the beach." He glanced at his brightly flowered shirt and the sandals on his feet. "Oh, yeah. I *am* a dude. Forgot that for a second."

Tim laughed at his own joke, but neither Max nor Paige found it humorous. Instead Max's attention was focused solely on how nervous and upset Paige was. He wished Tim would leave them alone, which he did a minute later when a friend of his entered the café.

As soon as Tim was out of hearing range, Max said to Paige, "Sounds like one of those guys who come in here all the time just to flirt with you."

Paige didn't seem convinced. "I wish I knew for certain who it was."

Max would call Travis in a couple of minutes and see if anything new had happened in the last few hours. But if Brad's goons were still trying to break into their office, that meant they didn't know where Paige was. Max had serious doubts that they could have figured it out since last night.

But he couldn't take any chances.

"Don't worry," he told Paige, hoping to comfort her. "I'm sure it was nothing serious."

She nodded, but seemed completely unconvinced. "I guess I'll get to work." But she'd only taken a couple of steps when she turned back toward him and asked, "Can you come home with me tonight? There's something I want to tell you. Something I think you should know."

"Sure," he said, trying to be casual. "Is it something you can tell me now?"

"No. But I need to be honest with you," she said. "I owe it to you."

He tensed, guessing what she was going to say next and not wanting to hear the actual words.

"I need to tell you the truth. It's the least I can do since you've been honest with me," Paige said.

Ah, damn.

Max glanced at his watch. He had a couple of minutes before his shift started, so he slipped into the stockroom and called Travis.

This wasn't good. Paige was about to tell him the

whole story because he was such an honest, forth-right guy.

And when she told him this news, when she poured her heart out to him, what was he going to do? He was going to look her dead in the eye and lie like crazy. Could a man get any lower?

When Travis finally answered, he sounded distracted. All he said was, "Nine. Later." Then he hung up.

Max stared at his phone. Something was wrong. Really wrong. Nine was their code word for everyone was okay, but that something had happened. It also meant the other person couldn't talk right now. So now Max had to wait until the promised "later" to talk to Travis and find out what was wrong. He knew better than to rush his brother. Trav would do what he had to do, then the second he could, he'd let Max know what was happening.

But Max had never been good at waiting. He was an action kind of guy. He wanted to take charge and handle the problem. Sometimes in this business, though, waiting was the best course of action. Now was one of those times.

Knowing it probably would be some time before Travis called back, Max headed to the bar.

"I need four beers and a cola," Paige said, bypassing Tim and bringing her order to him.

"Sure thing," Max said, getting to work. He glanced at Paige, and as usual, he felt happy just to be near her.

He knew he was becoming a sap, but he couldn't help it. "How's your night going?"

She was jotting down some notes, but now she looked up at him and smiled that sweet, sexy smile of hers he really liked. "I'm great. I'm making a few more notes about the festival. How's your night going?"

He couldn't tell her about Travis and how much that had rattled him. Instead he said, "It's going great, now that I've gotten to see you."

She rewarded him with a wink. "I feel the same way. Always brightens my world."

As she walked away, Tim wandered over and slapped Max on the back. "She's in love with you, buddy boy."

Max froze and stared at Tim. "What?"

"Paige. Loves. You." Tim said each word slowly, his grin so wide it was almost too big for his face.

"No, she doesn't. I mean, we're involved, but that's all." Max moved away from the other man, shaking his head as he went. Tim was wrong. Dead wrong. Paige wasn't looking for anything long-term any more than he was. She knew this wasn't going anywhere. They were just enjoying each other's company. That was it.

"She's not in love," he repeated. "We care about each other. But it's not love."

Tim narrowed his eyes. "Maybe not yet. But soon, and you're fooling yourself if you think you're not falling, too."

Max knew Tim was hoping he'd confide in him, but

there was zero chance of that happening, so he just moved farther away.

"You're wrong." Max started refilling the snack bowls.

Tim wasn't easily discouraged. He came over and stood next to Max again. "Do you always delude yourself this way, because it isn't healthy. You need to face reality, Max."

"Not funny."

"Okay, but don't say I didn't warn you." He gave Max a look that could only be described as paternal. "I feel responsible for her because I hired her, and then convinced her to stay on when she wanted to quit about six weeks later."

That was news to Max. He hadn't realized Paige had thought about running from Key West. "Why did she want to leave?"

"Said she couldn't stay in one place too long. At the time I thought she meant she got bored easily and liked to move around. But now I get the feeling there's a lot more to this than I realized."

So Paige had wanted to move on? He couldn't help wondering why she hadn't. He asked Tim what he thought, and the other man laughed.

"Emilio and I, along with the rest of the employees, all hounded her to stay until she finally changed her mind. I think she didn't realize how many friends she had here. It seemed to really mean a lot to her."

Friends. Yes, Max could understand how much that

meant to Paige after she'd spent months on her own trying to get away from Brad.

Max also knew she now thought that Brad wasn't after her anymore, which unfortunately he knew wasn't true.

"That's nice that you convinced her to stay," Max said when he realized Tim was watching him closely.

"I recognize good people when I meet them." Tim kept his gaze fixed on Max. All trace of his usual humorous personality was gone. This was a man with a mission, so Max let him talk.

"For instance, take you. You're a good guy. Oh, I know you're not quite who you say you are but—"

Max cut him off. "What do you mean by that?"

Tim sighed. "Please. Don't bother to protest. And I don't care what it is that you're hiding. All I care is that you take care of Paige. I know you wouldn't hurt her yourself. But now I need something more from you. I need you to promise me you'll keep other people from hurting her as well. In return, I won't pry into whatever deep dark secret it is you're hiding." Tim extended his right hand. "Deal?"

Max briefly considered protesting, but finally realized why bother. Tim was right. He had good people instincts. He'd sized up Max and Paige really well despite neither of them telling him the truth.

Max shook the other man's hand. "I guarantee I won't let anything bad happen to Paige. You have my promise."

For a moment, Tim studied him. Then he nodded.

"Good. I knew she could count on you for more than merely amazing sex."

With a groan, Max walked away. "Jeez, will you let that go?"

Tim was back to his old self again. "Never," he said with a laugh. "In fact, I think I'll go tease Paige about it. Man's got to find diversion where he can." He hollered at Paige and headed out to the patio.

Max watched as the other man followed Paige around, teasing and asking questions, which only made her laugh. He liked listening to the sound of her laughter. Paige had a great laugh, full and rich.

The vibrating of his cell phone pulled his attention away from Paige. Since it was slow, Max signaled Tim, who nodded and came over to watch the bar.

"Be right back," Max said, heading outside. He wanted to make certain no one overheard this call.

He headed toward his car. There he could talk in private and still keep an eye on the café.

"What's up?" he asked his brother.

"Someone broke in," Trav said. "I left for a short meeting, and when I got back, the place was trashed."

"You okay?"

"I'm fine, but Max—"

"Paige's file was stolen, right?" Max sighed, already knowing the answer.

"Yeah, but don't worry. I didn't record any of the info about where you are. And since you drove to Florida, it's not like they can trace your plane flight."

Max drummed his fingers on the steering wheel.

Okay, so they'd gotten the file, but that didn't mean they knew where Paige was.

A sudden thought hit him. "Trav, eleven," he said, resorting to another of their codes.

"Max, I don't think..." Travis stopped talking. "You think eleven is the right time? Seems kind of late."

Max sighed and ran one hand through his hair. "I think eleven is exactly right."

"Okay," Travis said, and then he hung up. Max waited impatiently for his brother to call him back, but it took some time for the phone to ring. Travis would be heading outside so he could call on his cell phone without worrying about being overheard.

"I think the office is bugged," Max said as soon as his brother called back.

"I already thought of that, so I took the office phone apart and looked the place over, but I didn't find anything. Sure you're not giving them more credit than they deserve? They tore the place apart, which wasn't smart. It let me know they'd been there. If they'd been smart, they would have tried to make it look untouched."

Max only wished these guys were dumb, but he knew better. He knew not to underestimate them. Brad Collier could afford the best, and Max was operating under the assumption that the best was exactly who he'd hired.

"You still would have known they'd been there, and they know that. They also know that this way, the cops will think it was random smash and trash. Let me guess, they took a couple of computers. The police probably said whoever had broken in had done so because they wanted something to hock for drug money, right?"

Travis laughed, but it wasn't a joyful sound. "Yeah. Of course, I denied that we were working on a case that would result in this sort of thing. That left them with no other conclusion to draw than it was a routine burglary."

Max studied a group of typical Key West tourists entering the café. Now it came down to him. He was positive the office was bugged, and Travis had mentioned he was in Florida before he'd stopped him. That meant they knew a lot more than they'd known this morning. It wouldn't take long to find Paige.

Travis must have been thinking along the same lines. "You going to get her to move? Maybe you could shift her to the Midwest."

"I don't think she'll go," Max told him. "We have this thing at work coming up. It's some sort of festival and Paige has put a lot of work into it."

"Well, you'll just have to convince her to forget about it."

"I may have a chance. I think she plans on telling me what's been happening with Collier and why she's here in Key West."

Travis was silent for a couple of seconds. Then he said, "Seems like a heck of a confidence to share with a co-worker. Want to tell me what's really going on down there?"

Max might be lots of things, but he wouldn't lie to his brother. They'd been through too much in their lives. All those Army bases. All those new schools. They'd always been each other's best friend. The one who always understood. He could tell Travis anything.

But not this. Not what was happening with Paige. Trav wouldn't understand, because frankly, he didn't understand, either.

So he told his brother the only truth he could, "I have everything under control."

He expected Travis to make a comment. His brother was smart and probably knew exactly what was happening. If he'd been in Travis's place, Max imagined he'd let his brother have it. He'd warn him about the danger of getting involved with a client. He'd warn him about losing focus and not giving one hundred percent to the job.

Max was thankful Travis was a different type of person. All his brother said was his usual, "CYA."

But that was enough.

Paige spent most of the night trying to figure out how to tell Max about Brad. How exactly did you say something like that? Dinner was great, the dessert was fabulous, oh and I think I'm being stalked by a crazed ex-fiancé?

Using the right words was very important. She needed to tell Max what was happening. Even though they'd agreed what they were sharing was short-term, he needed to know about the danger he could be in.

Sure, more than likely that man who'd called was a Sunset customer who wanted to hit on her. But she couldn't be certain, which meant she couldn't put off telling Max any longer.

Of course, there was a risk to telling him. Max might decide she wasn't worth it. But she'd have to take that risk. It was the right thing to do.

By the time their shift was over and they were in Max's car, Paige's nerves were raw. She still didn't know how to tell him, but she was certain telling him was the right thing to do.

So much so that the second they pulled out of the Sunset's parking lot, she said, "I've been debating all night whether I should tell you this. I can't help worrying that you'll want to stop seeing me after you know what's going on."

Max glanced at her. "Nothing you tell will make me want to stop seeing you."

Well, that was encouraging. "Sure?"

"Positive. Like I said, you don't know everything about me, either, but it shouldn't matter. Right?"

She nodded. "Right."

"So tell me what's on your mind."

Paige shifted in her seat so she was somewhat facing him. "Okay, here goes. I'm being chased by my ex-fiancé. His name is Brad Collier. He's a successful financial management consultant, and he's the son of an Illinois senator. I've spent the last year moving around the country. I've lived several places, but each time he's found me. Except for here in the Keys. I've been here several months now and nothing's happened."

Max was silent for a second. Then he asked, "Why is he chasing you?"

"That's the whole mystery," she admitted. "I have no idea. Truthfully, I'm not one hundred percent sure he's still chasing me. But he was at one point. He's even sent goons after me. I can't imagine he'd do this just because he's mad I called off the engagement, but I also can't figure out what's going on." She didn't want to ask the next question, but she had to know. "So do you hate me?"

He immediately shook his head. "Of course I don't hate you. But I'd like to meet this Brad guy in a dark alley. In fact, I think I should have a talk with him."

"No, don't do that. I don't want him to know where I am."

Max turned onto the street where her apartment was, then asked, "So how long are you going to hide from him?"

Paige was glad he was taking this well. He didn't seem shocked or upset at all. "I don't know. Nothing's happened since I came to Key West. I think he may have given up."

"But you're not sure, and you can't take the chance he hasn't," Max said. "I think you'd better keep a low profile until you know for sure. In fact, since you've been in Key West so long, maybe you should consider moving on to a new place soon."

Wow, that surprised her. She hadn't expected him to

suggest she move, and she couldn't help wondering if his suggestion was a polite way to get her out of his life. "Why would you think I'd need to move again?"

He didn't answer at first. Instead he waited until he'd parked at her apartment, then he said, "Because I don't want anything to happen to you. I want you to be very careful, and I can't help thinking maybe you'd be better if you moved again. You said yourself that up until you moved here, you'd never stayed in one place very long. But you've been in the Keys for several months now. He might be getting close to finding you again."

Paige frowned. She didn't like to think that, but then again, Max might have a point. She thought about his suggestion for a moment, then reminded herself that nothing had happened since she'd come to Key West.

So why should she move again? She liked it here.

"I don't want to leave," she admitted. "For a lot of reasons, starting with we have the festival coming up this weekend."

"Not worth risking your life for," Max said.

"But he hasn't found me." Paige opened her door and headed toward the stairs. "I'm still safe here."

When they got to her apartment, Max unlocked the door. Once they were inside, he turned to face her, his expression serious.

"How can you be certain he hasn't found you or isn't getting close?" Max sighed. "It's like I keep saying in self-defense class—be smart, be safe. You need to do whatever has to be done to stay safe."

She wasn't sure why he was pushing her so hard about moving. Well, unless...

"Is this your way of saying you'd rather we not see each other anymore?" she asked.

"Not at all. In fact, if you leave, I want to go with you."

With her? That didn't sound like something someone did when they were involved in a short-term relationship.

"Max, I really don't think there's any reason for me to leave Key West yet. I don't think he's found me. For all I know, he isn't even looking for me anymore."

Max sat on the couch, and Sugar immediately jumped into his lap. Paige hadn't missed that her dog was more than a little in love with the man.

"I'll tell you what," he said. "Let me have someone I know check up on this Collier guy. He can find out what's going on. Then we'll know if you need to move again."

His plan sounded reasonable, but still, Paige didn't think it was necessary.

"I feel safe here," she assured him. "Besides, you're teaching me how to defend myself."

"Self-defense moves can only do so much," he said.

Paige sat next to him on the couch. "Okay. Have that friend of yours check up on Brad. Maybe then we'll know if I should move."

"Okay." Max continued to pat Sugar. "I'm glad you told me."

Paige gave him a quick smile, then said, "Oh, and there's something else."

"More?"

"Yes. My name isn't really Paige Harris."

He stopped patting the dog and looked at her. "No?"

"Well, not really. Paige is my middle name and when I was growing up, my mom called me Paige. But my name is actually Alyssa Delacourte. Harris is my mother's maiden name. I wanted to make it at least a little difficult for Brad to find me."

"Seems smart."

"I didn't change my name at first, and that made it too easy for him," she explained. She studied Max for a second, trying to judge how he felt about everything she'd told him. But he looked fine. More than fine. He wasn't upset or shocked at all.

"So what do you want me to call you? Paige or Alyssa?"

"I love it when you call me Paige. My mom used to call me that."

Max leaned over and kissed her softly. "Good, because I've gotten used to thinking of you as Paige."

"I'm just glad you're not upset," she said.

Max frowned. "Why would I be upset?"

"Because I've been lying to you."

For a second, he simply looked at her. Then he said slowly, "You had a really good reason. That's what matters."

"Maybe." She liked that he thought that, and gave

him a kiss for being so sweet about everything. Not surprisingly, one kiss soon turned into another, and before she had a chance to say anything else, she'd pretty much forgotten what they'd been talking about.

8

MAX FINISHED SETTING the last paper cup on the floor, and then looked at the crowd assembled for the self-defense class. This was his fifth class, and he was glad he'd done this. He might not have taught them any more than the basics of protecting themselves, but at least it was something.

"One of the main ways you can hurt an attacker is to stomp on his instep," Max told the group.

"Or hers," Emilio piped in. "Not all attackers are men."

"Oh, puhlease. Most of them are," Tim said, putting his hands on his hips. "I want to know how to kick the butt of some big guy."

"You can't," Emilio said. "The best you can hope for, Tim, is that you run faster than he does."

"I can't run very fast," Krystal said. "I guess I'm out of luck."

"I'm fast, but I run funny." Annie looked at Max. "Will that cause me problems?"

Max bit back a chuckle and glanced at Paige. He could tell she was trying hard not to laugh as well.

Clearing his throat, he said, "I'm sure each of you can run fairly fast, or you will if you're being chased.

But what I'm going to show you right now is how to stomp on a guy—" He looked at Emilio. "A *person's* instep with enough force to cause intense pain."

"Why the paper cups?" Tim nodded toward all the cups Max had spread around the room. "Why don't we practice stomping on each other's insteps?"

"Because you won't stomp hard since you won't want to hurt them. And I want you to get used to putting all your weight behind it."

"So what do we do?" Tim grinned. "Does the person who stomps the most win a prize? Hey, you could have this at the Midsummer's Night Extrava—oops, Festival."

Max shook his head. "Not going to happen, Tim."

"What is going to happen at this festival?" Emilio asked. "You and Paige are being very secretive."

"Because we want you to be surprised," Paige said. "Now why don't we concentrate on our lesson?"

"She's changing the subject," Tim said. "Can't be good."

"I bet they're planning a tea party." Emilio sighed. "I can see it now."

"Hey, it's not a tea party," Paige said. "For your information, it's going to be great."

Max decided to stop this conversation before it got completely out of hand. He did the only thing he knew for a fact would work—he stomped on one of the cups hard.

The loud pow noise brought all conversation to an end.

"Jeez, let us know when you're going to do something like that," Tim said, his hand against his heart. "I could have had an attack."

"Stomp," Max ordered.

The class did exactly what he asked, and for the next couple of minutes the noise level was deafening. Finally, once all the cups were smashed, Max walked them through some steps to break a hold, how to create a diversion, and how to lurch suddenly to surprise the attacker and get ready access to stomp on his instep.

Despite all the joking and laughter, by the time class was over, he knew that they'd all learned some helpful maneuvers that should help keep them safe.

Now if he could only convince Paige she wasn't safe in Key West. In the two days since she'd told him about Brad, he'd brought the subject up repeatedly, but she kept refusing to even consider moving. She kept telling him it was because she wanted to stick around for the festival, but he knew it was more than that.

Paige was happy here. She liked these people; she liked the life she'd created.

And sadly, she was convinced Brad Collier was no longer chasing her. But Max knew better. He just didn't know how to tell her. He'd tried saying his friend had discovered Brad was still very much interested in her location, but she'd shrugged and said it didn't matter. She was convinced he'd never find her.

Deciding to do what he could to keep her safe, Max walked over to Paige and spent some extra time showing her how to break free from an attacker.

"Hey, no fair groping your girlfriend while you're supposed to be teaching a class," Tim said with a laugh that was more of a hoot. "Grope her on your own time."

"Ha, ha," Max said. "Very funny." He turned and looked at the class. "We're done here today, but always remember, the best thing you can do is avoid an attack in the first place. If you sense danger, or even if there's only the remote possibility of danger, you need to protect yourself."

Paige looked up at him and he could clearly tell from her expression that she knew he was talking to her. Yeah, well, he was. He wanted to move her someplace safe. The festival wasn't important. All that mattered was her safety.

Now he just had to figure out a way to get her to listen to reason.

"I'm fine," she said to him.

"You would be if you moved," he countered.

"We can talk about this after the festival," she said. "We've put too much work into it to run away now."

"Who's running away?" Tim came over to stand next to them. "Does this have to do with Krystal not being a good runner while poor Annie runs funny? If it does, then I'd better admit I probably run funny, too."

"No one is talking about running," Paige told him. "We're talking about the festival."

"Goody. Tell me what you're planning. I've noticed all the tables and chairs you've been stockpiling. Whatcha going to do with them? Did Krystal's body painting idea make the final cut?''

Tim looked so needy for information that Max would have told him a little bit of the plans if Paige hadn't sworn him to secrecy. She wanted the festival to be a big surprise, so she didn't want to tell anyone anything.

"You'll have to come to the festival and find out for yourself," Paige told him.

"I'm not sure I like you anymore," Tim teased. "I always thought of you as sweet, but now I'm finding out you have a really mean side to your personality."

Paige laughed. "Thanks. I like to think I can be tough when the occasion calls for it."

"Too tough," Tim complained, wandering off and telling the others that he hadn't been able to learn a thing.

"Do you think I'm being too mean?" Paige asked.

"No. I think you're being too careless."

Paige rolled her eyes. "Are you going to harp on that constantly between now and the festival on Saturday?"

Max told her the truth. "Yes. I am."

For a second, they simply looked at each other. Max knew she thought he was overreacting, but he wasn't. She was in danger, and he wanted to keep her safe. No, he *needed* to keep her safe. This had long since stopped being a normal job for him, and Paige wasn't a normal client. He cared about her. Cared a lot about her. And the thought of someone hurting her made him crazy.

So, yeah. He was going to keep harping on this.

With a sigh, she finally said, "If I swear on your brother's head to seriously consider moving after the festival on Saturday, will you drop the subject for the next couple of days?"

Max knew that was the best offer he was going to get, so he reluctantly agreed.

"Fine. But as soon as the festival is over, you and I are having a serious talk."

She stood up straight and gave him a mock salute. "You betcha, sir."

Max smiled. "Cute."

With a sexy little smile, she said, "Yeah, I think you're cute, too."

Then she walked over to join Krystal and Annie. Max watched her go, hoping he hadn't made a big mistake by agreeing to let it go for a few days.

What if they didn't have a few days? Something really bad could happen at any time.

PAIGE BLINKED and looked around. Good, Max was back in bed. In the little over a week since they'd become lovers, she'd gotten so she had trouble sleeping when he wasn't beside her. So much so that a couple of hours ago, she'd woken up when she'd rolled over and discovered he wasn't there. She went exploring and found him in the kitchen talking on the phone to his brother.

He'd been so sweet about the whole thing. He'd immediately asked if she'd heard him talking. She liked that he thought about her comfort and obviously worried about waking her. But she'd assured him he hadn't, and they'd gone back to bed.

For a split second, she considered waking him and showing him once again how much he meant to her. But as she watched him sleep, she decided to leave him be.

The poor man seemed exhausted. He was sleeping so deeply she decided she wouldn't disturb him if she slipped out of bed. She wanted something to eat. All of the exercise they'd had last night had really made her hungry.

Carefully she moved the arm he'd thrown over her and slipped to the side of the bed. Max sighed, and for a second she thought he would wake up, but then he settled down again.

Most men looked soft and kind of like teddy bears when they were asleep, but not Max. He lost none of his sexiness, not one bit of that raw maleness that made her so attracted to him. Even now, sound asleep, he looked strong enough to tackle the world.

And she was so glad he'd come into her life. He was unlike any other man she'd ever met, and even though the circumstances of her life right now made it complicated, she was glad they'd decided to be together. Even if it was only for a short time.

As she headed to the kitchen, Paige couldn't help thinking maybe that short-term agreement they'd originally reached wasn't going to be necessary for much longer. If it turned out that Brad wasn't chasing her, then there was no reason she couldn't resume a normal life.

A normal life that could easily include Max.

When she reached the kitchen, Sugar climbed out of her small bed and trotted over to Paige.

"Are you hungry, too?" She glanced at the clock. "It's only five in the morning and we're both starving." She rooted around in the refrigerator. "Slim pickings, Sugar. I need to go to the grocery store."

Of course, that meant giving up some of her free time, and she'd much rather be with Max.

She dug farther back in the fridge. "Ha, eggs. Success."

Sugar pranced, obviously sensing something good was going to happen.

"Calm down, I haven't managed to cook them yet. I could still mess this up," she teased the dog.

But Sugar seemed to have the utmost faith in her because she continued to yip and yap with great excitement.

Paige pulled out a frying pan and was debating how to cook the eggs, when she noticed Max had left his cell phone on the counter. It was sweet that he and his brother were close. It must be nice to have a sibling. Family was so important. She'd never been close to her father, and the last few months would do nothing to improve that relationship.

Of course, she was close to her grandmother. Alma Harris was seventy going on eighteen. She still traveled a lot with her friends, still enjoyed seeing the world.

Her grandmother had been the only one to believe her when she'd explained about Brad. Alma had even tried to convince Paige to stay with her while they sorted this out. But Paige had stayed at her grandmother's house for a couple of days when this whole mess had first started, and someone had tried to break in. She couldn't put her grandmother in that kind of danger, so she'd left.

Paige still felt that had been the right thing to do, but after all these months, she really missed the older woman. She glanced at the clock. Her grandmother should be getting up about now. She always awoke with the dawn and practiced her yoga in what she called the day's first smile.

Paige glanced again at Max's cell phone. She tried not to call anyone she knew just in case Brad figured out a way to trace her, but what harm could there be in using Max's phone? There was no way it could be traced.

And she really did want to talk to her grandmother, wanted to hear her familiar voice. Being with Max had reminded her how much of her life she'd let Brad take away from her. He'd stolen her family, her friends, and her security. Calling Nana would help her get another small bit of her life back.

Luck was with her. Her grandmother was home and answered on the first ring.

"Kenneth, I'm getting lonely," her grandmother said. "Hurry over here now."

Paige laughed at her grandmother's combination plea and order. Kenneth was Nana's best friend, and over the years, Paige had suspected the elderly gentleman was a lot more than just a friend.

"Hey, I'm not Kenneth!"

"Paige," Alma practically screamed. "Honey, I'm so glad to hear from you. Are you okay? Did you handle that boyfriend of yours? If not, come on back here. Kenneth and I will protect you."

Paige smiled at the ferocious tone in her grandmother's voice. She really loved and admired the older woman, and for that reason, wouldn't put her in danger.

"Nana, I can't talk long, but I wanted you to know how much I love you and that I've been thinking about you."

Her grandmother made a tsking noise. "You're still running from that man." She lowered her voice, although Paige had no idea why. "Listen to me, Kenneth can help you take care of that hoodlum."

Her offer was very sweet and well intentioned, but Paige loved her grandmother too much to risk her life.

"Thanks, but I'm fine."

"Where? Where are you, honey?"

Paige wanted to tell her, but she realized she shouldn't, so all she said, "It's one of your favorite places."

Her grandmother made a snorting noise. "That's no

help. There are many places I love. I love Paris. Are you there?"

"No, definitely not Paris, but Nana, I should be going. I'm—"

"Um, I guess London is out of the question, too." There was a long pause, and then she said, "I just hope it's someplace with a lot of sun. You need sun in your life during these dark days."

Her grandmother was a great believer in using the world around you to help cure your problems. Truthfully, that's why Paige had chosen Key West. Her grandmother always raved about the city and the sun, so when things had seemed bleakest to Paige, she'd taken her grandmother's advice and headed toward the sun.

"There's lots of sun," Paige assured her.

With a soft laugh, Alma said, "I think I know where you are, honey, and I'm happy you're there. I love that place, and I know the sun will help you see clearer."

Paige wasn't quite sure what her grandmother meant by that, but she would agree that Key West had been good to her. She'd met Max here, and despite everything, she'd never regret that.

"Don't worry," Paige said, knowing she'd already talked too long. "I'll be fine."

"Of course you will. You're my granddaughter. You'll find a way. I know you will. I love you, too."

Paige felt her throat tighten at her grandmother's concern. She missed the older woman and couldn't wait until she could go see her again, until this whole miserable mess was over and she could reclaim her life.

"I love you, too," she said. She heard the faint sound of a doorbell ringing at her grandmother's house. "I think Kenneth is finally there."

Alma made a kissing noise. "Here's luck coming your way, honey. Lots of luck. And remember, always face toward the sun. It will help you find peace." Then she said, "Kenneth, I'm coming, hold on."

Smiling, Paige said goodbye and hung up. She was glad her grandmother had someone special in her life, someone she cared about.

Paige set Max's phone back on the counter, and then started breakfast. In addition to the eggs, she sliced a couple of oranges she found, and headed back to the bedroom.

She wanted to be with Max.

MAX FINISHED PUTTING the table together and placed it in the tent in the corner of the parking lot like Paige's diagram depicted. There. That was the last of them. He'd put together all the tables, unloaded all the chairs, and gotten the twinkle lights ready to hang in the morning.

"Good job, Walker," he told himself.

"Have I reduced you to talking to yourself?" Paige asked with a laugh as she crossed the parking lot.

Max smiled as he watched her approach. Seeing Paige always made him smile.

"Yeah, I think it's gotten that bad," he told her.

When she was even with him, she leaned up and gave him a long, lingering kiss.

"Not that I'm complaining, but what was that for?" he asked when she finally broke the contact.

"A reward for my macho man who had to assemble all these folding tables all by himself with his two bare hands."

Max chuckled. "Okay, I guess I deserve that."

"Actually you deserve a round of applause for how hard you've worked to make this festival come about," she told him. "I couldn't have done it without you."

"Not true. This is your baby, Paige. You put it together. All I did was—" He waved at the tables and chairs. "Assemble a few pieces of furniture."

Paige started to disagree, but this time, he was the one to end the conversation with a kiss. Unlike her kiss, he took his time, exploring her lips with great care.

He was still kissing her when the hollering from the door to the Sunset finally caught his attention. Reluctantly he lifted his head and looked at Tim.

"What?" Max yelled. "I'm busy."

"I told you before, grope each other on your own time. Right now you're supposed to be putting together the festival so the rest of us can have some fun, too," Tim yelled back.

"Ogre," Max shouted back.

"Cad," Tim returned.

Max looked down at Paige, who was grinning. "Tim sure knows how to spoil a good time."

"At least now you're a cad. That's better than a Neanderthal."

Max turned the words over in his mind, and then shook his head. "Naw, that's a lateral move. A cad's just a Neanderthal wearing better clothes."

She laughed. "You may have a point there." Then with a sexy, little smile, she promised, "We'll pick up that kiss later."

Oh, yeah. Definitely later.

They were halfway across the parking lot when Max's cell phone rang. A quick glance told him it was Travis.

"It's my brother," he told Paige.

She nodded, and then said, "Tell him I said hi."

He hesitated, and she laughed. "Okay, don't tell him I said hi. I take it he doesn't know who I am."

"Yes, he does." The phone kept ringing, so he pushed the talk button and said, "Hold on a sec."

"He knows who I am?" She seemed really pleased to hear that. "You've talked to Travis about me?"

"He's the one who checked on Brad," Max explained, hoping he didn't have to go into any more detail than that.

Paige had taken a few steps toward the Sunset, but now she spun and walked back to him. "Mind if I say hi?"

Max wasn't sure what to say. He knew Travis would be smart enough not to blow his cover, but it had never occurred to him that Paige would want to talk to his brother.

"Uh, well—" he said.

She held out one hand. "Let me say hi. I promise I won't embarrass you. It's just I want to talk to the man on whose head I've been making all sorts of promises."

With his gaze still on Paige, Max said into the phone, "Paige wants to say hi."

He could hear Travis talking, but he couldn't make out what his brother was saying as he placed the cell phone into Paige's hand.

"Be gentle," Max warned her. "He frightens easily."

Paige laughed and said into the phone, "Hello, Travis. It's nice to finally sort of meet you."

Max would give anything to know what his brother was saying to Paige. Whatever it was, it kept making her laugh. No doubt he'd never hear the end of this from Travis.

After what seemed like an eternity, Paige said, "I'm really glad we had this chance to talk. I enjoyed it."

Then, with a teasing smile, Paige handed the phone back to Max. "See you inside."

As soon as Paige was out of hearing range, Max lifted the phone. "Okay, what did you say to her?"

"My, my. She must be a really special client if you let her talk to your brother on the phone," Travis said, sounding way too smug for Max's peace of mind.

"Very funny. What did you say to her?"

Travis laughed. "Calm down. Nothing bad. I told her as brothers went, you weren't the worst one in the world."

"Gee, thanks," Max said dryly.

"She seemed to like it," Travis countered.

"Why did you call?"

"Oh, right." The humor faded from Travis's voice. "I've spent the morning with the police. They found the stuff stolen from our office. It was tossed in a Dumpster a few miles from here. Guess what was the only thing missing."

Max didn't need to guess; he knew. "Paige's file."

"You got it. Even the computer they took was tossed in the Dumpster. The police were baffled by that since they were convinced the burglars had taken the computer to sell it for drug money. But they tossed it. Just like they tossed everything else."

This confirmed his fears. They'd gotten what they wanted—information about Paige. "What was in the file?"

"I don't think there was anything that would lead them to you," Travis said, but he didn't sound any surer than Max felt. "But just in case, you'd better move her."

"Tomorrow. The festival is tomorrow. I'll move her as soon as that's over." That was, if he could convince her to go.

Travis sighed. "Fine. But let's hope for both your sakes that tomorrow is soon enough."

"Yeah, let's hope," Max said, knowing what could happen to Paige if he were wrong. But it wasn't like he had a choice. Paige wasn't about to leave before the festival tomorrow. The best he could do between now and then was watch her constantly.

Almost as if he'd read his mind, Travis said, "Keep a close eye on her, bro."

"I will," Max assured him. "I won't let her out of my sight."

9

"OKAY, I'LL ADMIT IT—this is the last thing I expected," Tim said, his hands on his hips, his mouth hanging open. "We've had some raunchy extravaganzas before."

"Yeah, we've had lots of them," Emilio added, his expression equally stunned.

"And we've had a few fairly average extravaganzas, too," Tim went on. "Hell, we even had a couple that were almost tame."

Paige bit back a smile. She knew Tim and Emilio were darn near speechless, which in itself was almost worth all the time, work, and effort Max and she had spent on this night.

"You once held a tame extravaganza? Hard to believe."

Max had wandered over to join them. He laughed when he heard her comment. "Yeah, I for one don't believe it."

"It's true," Tim said, still surveying the crowd. "But we've never had anything like this. Not in all those years."

This was A Night of Magic. She and Max had decorated the trees with tiny white lights, put up tents, hung lanterns all over the parking lot, and then invited all the local charities to set up game booths where guests could try magic tricks and win prizes.

The whole place had a fun, upscale carnival atmosphere and was pulling in people right and left. Even though it had just started, the parking lot was jammed.

Paige was thrilled. Not only had they fulfilled their promise to Tim and Emilio, but the local charities were going to make some serious cash off of tonight.

It really was a win-win situation.

"You two did good," Tim finally pronounced. "Very good."

"I've got food to cook," Emilio said. Then he hugged Paige. "But I agree with Tim. This is great."

After Emilio walked away, Paige glanced up at Max. He was looking at her in that sexy I'd-love-to-get-you-naked-way of his. She grinned at him, and he winked.

"You really need to credit Paige for this," he told Tim. "If it had been up to me, I think it would have been pizza, beer, and a rock band."

Paige was about to argue with him, but he did have a point. The theme of the party had been her idea. But he had pitched right in and helped once she'd explained what she'd had in mind.

"I couldn't have done it without Max," she said.

Tim looked from one to the other then said, "So now that you two are officially in love, does that mean we'll be hearing wedding bells soon?"

Stunned, Paige stared at him. She'd never even considered it.

"Of course not. Max and I are just..." She had no idea what to say. What were they? Lovers? Sure, but were they anything more than that?

She looked at Max, who didn't say a word. She could tell from his expression that he didn't know what to say, either. And who could blame him? He knew about Brad, and had to understand that until that situation was resolved, they couldn't decide what the future held for them if, in fact, it held anything at all.

Short-term. That had been their agreement up-front. Sure, she'd been thinking that maybe they could reconsider what they'd agreed on, but that was as far as she'd thought. She certainly hadn't given any thought to love. And definitely not to marriage.

"You're what?" Tim prompted when neither of them completed the sentence. "You have to finish, Paige. You two are what?"

"We're busy right now," she finally said in desperation, and then decided to get away before he could nudge her for any more information. "I think I'll go check on the booths."

Max fell into step with her. "I'll join you."

With a loud laugh, Tim said, "Okay, message received. I'll leave well enough alone and not pry. But just so you know, I think the two of you are cute as a button together."

"Gee, thanks," Max said, then he fell into step with Paige. "Nice to know Tim thinks we're cute."

She smiled and bumped against him. "That's because we are cute together."

"Yeah, I know it." He leaned down and kissed her lightly. Paige rose up on her toes, meeting his kiss and trying to woo him into lingering, but Max just chuckled.

"Later," he promised when he broke the kiss far too soon for Paige.

"I'm holding you to that." She threaded her fingers through his, and together, they wandered around the festival. She was proud of how her idea had come to life. Proud of what she'd accomplished here.

"You did good," Max whispered in her ear.

Paige completely agreed, but again she reminded him, "*We* did good."

Max was leaning down to whisper something in her ear when Krystal and Annie came running over.

"I can't believe what you've done," Krystal said. "This is amazing. Not at all what I expected."

"Does that mean it's not as boring as you expected?" Paige teased, knowing the other waitress had been figuring on the worst.

"It's not boring at all," Krystal said, sounding incredibly surprised.

"Do you get the feeling she didn't hold out much hope for us?" Paige teased Max.

"You do seem to have pleasantly surprised her," he said, and then laughed when Krystal pouted.

"Okay, okay. I was wrong. You didn't make it boring. Of course, it's not as exciting as it would have been if you'd invited the body painters, but it's still a lot of fun," Krystal said.

Annie nodded. "Definitely. And the people are flooding into the restaurant. I've picked up megatips tonight. Should be a banner night for everyone."

That's exactly what Paige wanted. She wanted the charities to make a lot of money and the café to do well. Based on the number of people pouring into the parking lot, it looked like she was going to get her wish.

She was scanning the crowd when she saw Diane weaving through the mass of people, her boyfriend Kyle in tow.

Paige waved at the other woman. "That's my friend, Diane, and her boyfriend, Kyle. I'd love for you to meet them."

"I've already met her," Max said. "She stopped me outside your apartment one day and gave me the third degree. I'll say this, she's very concerned about your well-being."

"She can be intense, but she's really very sweet," Paige said, curious as to what Diane would have asked Max. Based on his expression as he watched them approach, she'd bet Diane asked some tough questions.

When Diane and Kyle got even with them, Diane gave her a hug and said, "This festival is great, and you're a genius, Paige."

Paige was about to point out that Max had helped, too, when he said, "She did do a terrific job, didn't she?"

"We did," she said, nudging Max. "He doesn't want to take any of the credit, but he worked hard on this, too."

And he had. Despite everyone making a fuss over her, she couldn't have pulled off this festival without Max. She'd come up with the idea, but he'd done all the hard work to make the idea a reality.

"Paige, you didn't tell me you worked with your boyfriend," Diane said. Then she introduced Kyle to Max, her gaze never leaving Max's face.

"I told you I worked with Paige," Max pointed out. "The morning we met. You asked me specifically how I knew Paige, and I told you that we worked together."

"Hmm. I guess you did. I must have forgotten you'd said that," Diane said vaguely, but Paige didn't believe her. Diane was too sharp to have forgotten.

"I understand you asked Max a lot of questions when you met him," Paige said. "What sort of things did you ask?"

Kyle laughed. "Knowing Diane, she asked him everything from his shoe size to whether he wore contacts."

Diane made a huffy noise. "I asked nothing of the sort. For starters, I can tell he isn't wearing contacts, which means he either was born with good vision or he had his eyes operated on and now has good vision."

Unable to resist, Paige looked at Max's eyes. He winked at her, then said, "Born with perfect vision."

"See, so I didn't ask him everything, but since you mentioned it, there are a couple more questions I'd like to ask."

Kyle and Paige groaned, but Max chuckled. "Sure. Go ahead."

"Where were you born?"

Paige almost told Diane to stop, but then she realized she wanted to hear what Max said.

"Pensacola, Florida."

"You?"

Diane sighed. "Memphis. But I'm the one asking the questions."

"I'd be pretty rude if I didn't take an interest in you, too, since you're a friend of Paige's," he said with a grin that looked suspiciously smug. "Do you have any more questions?"

"Of course." She took a step closer to him. "How old are you?"

"Thirty-two. You?"

Kyle laughed again. "She's not going to tell you."

That remark earned him a frown from Diane, who then looked at Max and said, "Thirty-three."

Paige hadn't realized her friend was that old, and based on the somewhat surprised look on Kyle's face, she got the distinct feeling he hadn't known for certain how old Diane was, either.

He confirmed her thoughts when he said, "I thought you were thirty-one."

"You must have gotten confused," was all Diane said. Kyle gave his girlfriend a hug. "Doesn't matter to me if you're one hundred and thirty-three."

Diane's expression softened for a second while Kyle hugged her, but the second he released his hold, she went back to frowning at Max.

"What day were you born?

"Trying to figure out my sign?" When she didn't answer, he said, "April 7. I'm an Aries. You?"

"Capricorn. January 14."

Paige stared at her friend. "You know, you've told Max more about yourself in the last two minutes than you've told me in all the months we've known each other."

Diane looked partially self-conscious, but mostly determined. "I have a funny feeling about this guy." She looked at Max. "No offense."

Before Paige could protest, Max laughed and said, "None taken."

But there was no way Paige was going to let Diane get away with that. "Hey, you just insulted him. Diane, Max is a great guy."

"Yeah," Kyle said, nodding. "You insulted Max. Not nice, Diane."

"I said no offense," she repeated.

"That doesn't matter. You still were offensive." Kyle looked at Max. "Sorry about this. She's overprotective."

"She's also standing right here." Diane enunciated each word slowly. She managed to adopt an innocent expression, which wasn't easy considering she was doing everything but turning a spotlight on Max. "I didn't mean to offend him. I'm just...curious."

"Or snoopy," Kyle offered.

"Who me? I'm not doing anything."

"Of course you are," Paige said. "You're treating Max like a criminal."

Diane ignored her and instead asked Max. "Where do you live?"

Paige opened her mouth to tell Diane once again to cut it out, then suddenly realized she, too, had no idea where Max lived. He had a duffel bag with spare clothes and stuff that he carried in the back of his car so he'd never needed to go to his place to get things.

Funny, she'd never thought to ask him such a basic question, and as much as she hated to admit it, she wanted to hear what his answer was.

"Let the poor guy alone," Kyle said.

But Max made no protest and answered her question. "I haven't really found a place. Mostly I've been staying at a motel nearby."

"A motel?" Diane looked at Paige. "Have you been there?"

She wasn't about to admit she hadn't, and that in fact, this was the first time the question had come up. "Diane, stop. I appreciate you coming to the festival tonight, but Max and I are busy and need to go check on the booths."

Diane held up one hand. "One more question. You drive a black sedan, right?"

"Yes, I drive a sedan. And yes, it's black. But you know that since you've seen my car," Max said, his tone still polite although Paige imagined he was getting tired of being grilled like this.

Diane looked at Paige. "A *sedan*, Paige. He drives a sedan."

Oh, for crying out loud. "Diane, I'm not worried

about life in the suburbs, so I don't care that he drives a sedan."

"That's not why I'm asking, although you definitely should keep it in mind as you're making choices."

Max looked completely baffled as he said, "I'm sorry you don't like my car, but it gets good mileage."

Diane was staring at Max like he was a puppy kicker, and it made Paige cringe. She'd never seen her friend act this way before.

Enough was enough. "Cut it out," Paige told her.

Max had folded his arms across his chest and was studying Diane. "It's okay. I don't mind. Does it help if I tell you I really care about Paige and have no intention of hurting her?"

"Men say that all the time right before they break our hearts," Diane maintained.

Kyle looked at Max and sighed. "Sorry about this. She worries about her friends."

"You know what really worries me?" A rowdy crowd of festival-goers squashed by them, pushing Diane closer to Max. "Why was a black sedan parked across the street from our apartment building night after night weeks before you started seeing Paige. Were you spying on her, Max?"

No one said a word for a couple of seconds. Then Max laughed. "Of course not."

But there was something about his laugh that wasn't quite right. Diane and Kyle might not have noticed, but Paige did.

Still, she couldn't—and wouldn't—believe that Max had been spying on her. Diane had to be wrong.

"His car has been parked at our apartment complex for the last couple of weeks," she said. "Of course you've seen it."

"I know that. I'm talking about months ago. Long before you started to see Max," Diane said. She narrowed her eyes. "It used to sit across the street from our apartment complex. Tucked away, under some trees."

"Are you sure?" Kyle asked. "You never said anything to me about a car."

"I'm an artist. I notice the world around me," she said.

Rather than being offended, Max simply smiled. "I'm not sure what to tell you, Diane, but it wasn't my car. I've only been coming to your apartment complex since I've been dating Paige."

Diane started to say something else, but Kyle shot her a look, so she shrugged. "If you say so."

The tension level was sky high, and Paige struggled to think of a way to lessen it. Thankfully, one of the off-duty police officers they'd hired to help with traffic and the crowds stopped by to discuss a problem with Max.

"I'll catch up with you in a second," Max told Paige. He looked at Kyle and Diane. "Nice talking to you."

After Max walked away, Kyle shook his head. "That poor guy. You did everything but roast him on a grill."

"That man is lying to Paige big time," Diane said.

Paige hadn't expected that. "What?"

Diane sighed. "Put the pieces together. He lives in a *motel?* Why doesn't he have an apartment? If he's been in town for a couple of months and he plans on staying here, then why hasn't he found a place?" She patted Paige's arm. "You need to watch yourself around that one, Paige. Something isn't right."

"He probably doesn't have enough money to get an apartment just yet. The landlords always want so much money up-front, and he just got out of the service."

Diane didn't seem convinced. "You need to do some checking. You need to find out why this guy doesn't have a place to live. Is he expecting you to support him?"

"Of course not."

"Then what's the story? Is he lying and not planning on staying in Key West very long?" She leaned closer, obviously warming to the subject. "So then what happens to you once he leaves? He just dumps you and takes off, right, because what's to stop him?"

"Diane," Kyle said. "Let's go enjoy the festival."

She grabbed Paige's arm. "You haven't loaned him money, have you? That's probably what he's after, your money."

Paige almost laughed at that. She had no money, or at least she had none now. All of her money was sitting in a bank account waiting for Alyssa Delacourte to return. But Max didn't know about that money.

She'd told him about Brad but not about her family.

He had no way of knowing how much money her father had or about the trust fund she had.

Besides, she trusted him. "He's not after my money. Let it go."

"Men can fool you. Look at what's happening with Kyle, and I've been with him for years."

"To quote you, I'm standing right here," Kyle said. "And what's wrong with me?"

"The house," Diane said.

"Which you now love. Just wait till we move in." Kyle looked at Paige. "She loves her studio and she loves the house."

"That's beside the point," Diane maintained. "And let's not forget that I don't believe for a second that wasn't his car I saw. It was a dark sedan. I know what I saw."

"Max is a good guy. He isn't lying." Paige turned and surveyed the crowd. Surely there was something that needed her attention.

She didn't want to fight with Diane, but she trusted Max, completely trusted him. Okay, so she'd misjudged Brad, but she knew deep in her heart that she could trust Max. She was positive of that fact.

"I know you think you're helping, Diane, but I know what I'm doing."

"I hope so," Diane said softly, apparently worried Max might hear her. "Because when I looked at that sedan, I could have sworn the person was watching our building. I thought about calling the police, but the person inside didn't seem to be doing anything but sitting there. I never saw his face, but now I'm wondering if it was Max watching your apartment."

A sick feeling formed in Paige's stomach at even the thought of someone spying on her. Diane couldn't be right. Max wouldn't have spied on her apartment. He'd have no reason to do that.

Unless he'd been sent by Brad.

"Are you sure?" she asked Diane. "A lot of cars look alike."

Diane gave her a pitying look. "You just don't want it to be his car. But I keep telling you, I saw what I saw."

Paige felt cold. Diane seemed so certain. Turning, she scanned the crowd for Max. She'd expected to find him solving the problem, but instead, he was watching her from across the parking lot.

She met his gaze. Diane had to be wrong. Max couldn't be working for Brad. She was certain he wasn't, positive he was a good guy.

"Just be careful," Diane said as Kyle tugged on her arm.

"I think we've made enough trouble for one night," Kyle said. "Let's go visit the booths."

Paige was still looking at Max. She could feel her heart slamming in her chest, feel her breath catching in her throat. This couldn't be happening; it couldn't be true. Max wasn't working for Brad. She was positive he wasn't. But if that was the case, then why had he been watching her apartment? It didn't make any sense.

She continued to look at Max, trying to get her emotions under control. After a couple of seconds, he smiled at her. A sexy, caring smile, but rather than feeling better, Paige just felt worse.

She couldn't be wrong about him. Not about Max.

Could she?

10

DAMAGE CONTROL. Max knew he needed to do some serious damage control. He should have realized Paige would want to see his place at some point, but he'd been so focused on her, he'd screwed up. Again. Seemed like that was all he'd done on this case.

At least this was something he could handle. His first priority was to make certain Paige didn't grow suspicious of him. He needed her to trust him, and not just because of the danger Brad posed. He needed her trust for personal reasons.

But looking at her now through the crowd, he could tell he'd shaken that trust. Despite everything they'd shared, Paige was still jumpy. He watched her look away from him. Even from a distance he could tell that she was debating what to do.

Damn. How could he have been so stupid? He'd have to take care of this before something bad happened.

Max knew he'd have to get Paige alone and talk this over, but first they had to get through the festival. They couldn't just leave.

Still, he wanted to make things right, so he wove his

way through the crowd, his gaze never wavering from Paige's face.

As he got closer, she glanced at him, and then quickly glanced away. Ah, hell. This stuff with Diane had really shaken her confidence in him. He hated how she didn't meet his gaze when he got close.

"The Sleep Inn," he said when she looked like she might walk away. "I've been staying there because it's cheap and I'm poor."

Paige looked surprised and more than a little guilty. "I wasn't asking."

Oh, yeah, she was. The question was easy to read in her expression. "I didn't tell you where I live because I thought you'd think I was a loser. It's run-down, but it's a place to stay. I'm trying to save up enough to get a nice apartment."

That was true. Sort of. What stuff he didn't carry in his duffel was stowed in a matchbox-size room at the Sleep Inn, and if he'd had time, he would have found a better place to stay.

His explanation seemed to help, at least a little. Paige's expression softened. "You know I don't care how much money you have. I don't care where you live."

She seemed reassured by what he'd said. Good. At least he'd recovered somewhat.

The next problem was a bit tougher. To smooth this over, he needed to flat-out lie to her. "And I wasn't spying on you. I don't know what Diane is talking about."

Okay, not all of that was a lie. He hadn't been spying on her. He'd been protecting her. Watching over her.

Not spying.

But the big lie was that he knew precisely what Diane was talking about.

For a couple of seconds, Paige didn't say a thing. She just looked at him. When she did finally speak, her words came out quickly, almost as if she couldn't wait to get this conversation over. "I know it wasn't you parked outside. As soon as I thought it over, I realized it couldn't have been you. But I am worried that it might have been someone Brad sent."

He wasn't sure how many lies a man could tell in one night, but it looked like he was going to find out because he told Paige another one. "You could be right, which is why you need to leave here after tonight. That person watching your building could have been sent by Brad."

Paige looked uncertain. "I don't know. I don't want to move again unless I absolutely have to."

"Why don't we talk about it later tonight? I'll show you the motel I'm staying at, and we can think this through."

She nodded. "Sounds good."

Quickly deciding that the best defense was a good offense, Max said, "I just wish if Diane thought someone was spying on the apartment building that she'd called the police."

Paige nodded. "That would have been helpful, but I

doubt if it would have made Brad stop. Nothing seems to make him stop.''

Yeah, well something was going to make Brad Collier stop and that something was him. Once he got Paige someplace he knew was safe, he and Travis were going to change the rules of this game. He was tired of watching Paige be the mouse to Brad's cat. It was time to turn the tables on that scum.

The challenge was going to be convincing Paige to leave Key West. *That* wasn't going to be easy.

Or maybe it was because at that moment, Paige smiled softly at him. "I'm so glad you're here. Even knowing Brad could have found me isn't enough to ruin tonight."

Max felt like he'd won the lottery. Knowing how much Paige trusted him made him feel terrific. Those emotions that he kept trying to push away whenever he was around her were back in full-force. It was all he could do not to scoop her up in a big hug and kiss her until neither of them could stand up.

"I'm glad I'm here, too," he told her.

Whatever Paige might have said next was lost as the crowd started moving toward the large stage at the far end of the parking lot. The main attraction for the night was three master magicians, each of whom was going to put on a mini-show.

Max and Paige scooted over so they could be at the front. If a problem came up during the show, they'd have to be the ones to solve it.

The first magician was actually more of an escape

artist. He was tied in a straitjacket and locked in a safe that was then lowered into a pool of water. As the seconds ticked by, Max kept getting more and more nervous.

"I think I'd better rescue him," he finally said, heading toward the pool. In his mind he was already running through how he was going to get that safe open when a hand on his arm stopped him.

"I'm sure the guy is fine."

Max turned, and then laughed when he realized that the person who had spoken was the magician.

"Clever," he said to Paige as the man bounded onto the stage. "Sleight of hand. We're looking this way while he's doing something over there."

The next two magicians did equally good shows, but Max couldn't concentrate on them. He was focused on Paige. He couldn't shake the feeling that he needed to move her and soon.

When the show ended, several people came over to congratulate them on their hard work. It looked like the night was shaping up to be a big success. All of the charities were making money, the café was pulling in tons of people, and everyone was having fun.

For the rest of the night, Max stuck right with Paige. He didn't want to take any chances. Finally the crowd started to thin, and Tim wandered over.

"Tonight has been terrific," he said. "Really great idea."

"Thanks," Paige said.

"So why don't you two take off? Emilio and I will clean up this mess."

Normally Max would want to pitch in, but he wanted to take Paige to the motel. So when she glanced at him, he said, "Sounds great, Tim. Thanks."

After Tim walked away, he told Paige. "Come on. I want to show you this motel. It's cheap—I warn you."

Paige looked absolutely thrilled at the prospect. "You know it doesn't matter to me how much money you have."

He couldn't help laughing. She was so sweet. "It better not because I don't have a lot, but what I have I'll be happy to share with you."

She got that soft look on her face that meant she'd love to kiss him. That sounded like a great idea, but he wanted to wait until they got out of here.

It took a while, but finally, they were heading to his car. As they walked, he warned her, "Keep in mind that The Sleep Inn is kind of a dump. I'm going to show you my room to satisfy your curiosity, but don't expect much." Before she could answer, he added, "On second thought, don't expect anything at all. The place is a dive."

After they climbed into the car and were on their way, Paige shifted in her seat slightly so she was partly facing him. "Why would you think it would matter to me how much money you have? I don't have a lot of money, either."

Max barely bit back a laugh on that one. Alyssa Delacourte had plenty of money.

"It's a guy thing," was what he finally said.

Paige leaned over and kissed him on the cheek. "I'm not interested in your money. I'm interested in other things you have."

With a chuckle, Max said, "So I've noticed."

Paige leaned back in her seat. "Okay, I'm interested in *that*, but I'm also interested in your mind and your personality and your heart."

"Yeah, yeah, I know your type. You say you're interested in my mind, but you're only interested in me for my body. And now you're taking me to a shady motel, and you'll probably want to have your way with me."

Paige laughed, the sound light and sexy in the small car. "I like this plan. Go on."

Max was thrilled she was no longer suspicious of him. "Since it's a cheap motel, you'll probably be thinking there's nothing out of the question. That I'll be happy to do whatever you want however you want."

Even though he was teasing her, the thought of what they might share tonight was getting his blood pounding hard and heavy through his veins.

Paige apparently wasn't immune to the sensuous atmosphere in the car, either. Her voice was soft as she added, "I definitely get the feeling you're the kind of guy who's up for anything, any way, anytime. Am I right?"

He chuckled. "Up for anything. That's good. And yeah, you're right, if you're the lady in question." He pulled into the parking lot of the motel and parked in front of his room. Actually it was kind of a cottage.

He'd always thought of The Sleep Inn as kind of a run-down dumpy place, but looking at it now with its small bungalows, white twinkle lights in all the trees, and the sound of the ocean nearby, it kind of looked like an island retreat, the perfect place to have nuclear sex.

"This is cute," Paige said. "Very romantic and kind of exotic." She leaned toward him and whispered, "Exactly the right place to have a wild night with a wanton man."

Max surveyed the motel and made a mental note to never bring her here when the sun was out. Daylight wasn't a friend of the place. All of its flaws and problems were readily visible under that kind of scrutiny.

Kind of like him. As long as he kept her seeing only what he wanted her to see, he might be able to keep her safe.

But if he messed up and she saw who he really was, then he knew everything they shared, everything that had been happening between them, would disappear.

Tonight, though, he could maintain the illusion. He could be the perfect man she wanted so much, the one she trusted completely. And he would be. Tonight would be a night she'd remember forever.

"I'm going to tell you a story," he said as they climbed out of the car and headed up the stairs to his cottage. "It's about a beautiful woman and all the men who tried to win her heart."

He opened the door and kissed Paige. The kiss was wild and brazen. Again and again, he kissed her, pulling her tongue into his mouth and sucking, breathing in the very breath from her lungs.

As they kissed, he nudged them inside the room, kicking the door shut behind them. Then he buried his hands in Paige's hair and fed on the sweetness of her kiss. When she mewed softly, he kissed her deeper; when she rubbed herself against him, he held her closer. He loved the way his body meshed with Paige's, loved the way she felt in his arms. She was a part of him that he'd never known was missing.

When he finally ended the kiss, she looked dazed and excited. "Oh my."

He chuckled. "Yeah. Oh my." Reaching out, he took her hand and led her over to the bed. "Now where was I in my story? Right. The beautiful woman." He coaxed her down on the bed, his fingers caressing the soft skin of her arms in long, slow strokes.

"Um, what are you doing?" she asked, although he noticed her breathing had increased. He was getting to her.

"Trying to help you visualize the story. Now quiet." He continued to massage her arms. He leaned forward, and Paige leaned up, trying to kiss him, but he veered and rather than meeting her lips, whispered, "Every man wanted to please her. Every man wanted to win her heart."

Paige's lips parted and he lightly brushed them with his own, lingering just long enough to drive them both crazy. Then, as he held her gaze, he let his fingers slip under the hem of her T-shirt.

"Pleasing her was all the men thought about, all they wanted to do." He kept his touch light, sensual. Touching her like this was driving him crazy. All *he* wanted to do was bury himself deep within her, but this was better. A whole lot better.

Paige reached down and started to pull up her T-shirt, but he stopped her, moved her hands aside, and resumed caressing the sliver of skin he'd exposed above her shorts.

"The first man brought her riches, gold and silver and precious gems." He kissed her navel and dipped his tongue into the small indention.

"Um, Max, you are evil," she said, her breathing ragged. "Talented, but evil."

He chuckled and pushed her T-shirt up another couple of inches. "You have no idea. Now quiet. So the beautiful woman examined all of the riches, and what do you think she said?"

"I want to touch you," she murmured, tugging his T-shirt free from his jeans and caressing his back. "I want to run my hands over every square inch of your body."

Man, he liked the sound of that. But first, he wanted to do more for her.

"That's an excellent idea, but it's not what she said." He allowed himself to enjoy her touch for a few more seconds and then he moved away. There was only so much temptation a man could take.

"No, she sat and talked with the rich man and found

out that all he cared about, all he thought about, were his riches. After an hour, she sent him away."

"Smart lady," Paige said, raising her head and nibbling on his chin. "She knows money isn't the key to happiness, so it's good she told him to leave."

"True." Max pushed her shirt up, exposing her breasts. She was wearing a lacy bra that made his mouth go dry. He ran his fingers over her softness, watching as her nipples peaked.

"Max," she said on a sigh as he continued to caress her taut nipples through the silky fabric.

"She knew the rich man wouldn't make her happy since all he desired was his money." He skimmed his fingers over the tops of her breasts, and then returned his attention to her nipples. "He didn't truly desire her. He wanted to own her like a possession."

Paige tugged on his T-shirt and he let her remove it. She smiled like a kid with candy and ran her hands across his muscles. "Your chest is so sexy."

"I'm pretty fond of yours, too," he countered, flicking open the front clasp on her bra and peeling back the cups. "And it's definitely sexy."

He would have done more, but at the moment, Paige kissed his chest, her tongue doing phenomenal things on his skin. He never would have believed it was possible to be more aroused than he was at the moment, but she'd found a way to turn up the heat another notch.

"You're distracting me from my story," he said in a

last-ditch effort at keeping her from sending him over the edge.

She pulled off her T-shirt and bra, tossed them across the room, and then said, "By all means, continue."

Yeah, well that was easier said than done since all he could concentrate on at the moment were her breasts. Her taut pink nipples were begging him to touch them, taste them, and he obliged, lavishing both breasts with care and attention.

He got so distracted by her breasts that for a while, he didn't talk. He was much too busy for conversation. Finally he leaned back and surveyed her. She looked so sexy that it took all of his self-control not to end his little game right now.

But then she smiled at him and said, "So she decided she didn't want the rich man. What happened next?"

Thinking was fairly difficult at the moment considering all the blood in his body had left his brain and headed southward, but eventually, he told her, "The next man was the wisest man in the land. He brought her great knowledge."

He leaned over and took one taut nipple in his mouth and suckled. Paige sighed with pleasure, her hands running through his hair.

"I like smart men," she said. "They know a lot of fascinating things."

Max released her nipple and kissed the side of her breast. "That's true. They do know fascinating things.

But is that enough? Do you think that was enough for the beautiful woman?"

She leaned up and kissed him, her own hands wandering first over his chest, then down to the waistband of his jeans. "Intelligence is a great thing. It helps you be creative."

She snapped open his jeans. Then slid the zipper down inch by inch. "Creativity often can lead to pleasure."

Once she had his jeans open, she dipped her fingers inside the opening and wrapped her hand around his erection.

"Pleasure is a pretty powerful thing," he agreed, his voice raspy with passion. "But is it enough?"

Paige was caressing his length, her fingers trailing up and down and driving him crazy. "Hmmm, feels like more than enough to me."

Max would have laughed if he could have gotten air into his lungs. Instead he was focused on what she was doing to him.

"Take your pants off," she said, "then tell me the rest of your story."

She didn't need to ask him twice. He had his jeans and boxers off in a flash, and then slipped her shorts and panties off, too.

Joining her back on the bed, he trailed a hand down her abdomen, ending up in her soft curls.

"So you think the beautiful woman should have chosen the intelligent man because he was creative?"

Paige squirmed against his exploring fingers, moving even closer. "No."

She made an *eek* noise when he used his index finger to rub her most sensitive spot. She closed her eyes, and he could tell she was on the edge. To help her find the pleasure she craved, he leaned over and sucked hard on her right nipple.

Paige began to breathe quickly and move almost frantically beneath him. "Max," she said, her voice a whisper as she found the release she sought.

After she quieted, he gently kissed her lips. Emotion tugged at him. This woman meant so much to him. She was more than a client, more than someone he needed to protect. He'd grown to care deeply for her.

She opened her eyes and smiled at him. "Wow."

"Glad you liked it. Then you'll understand the rest of my story." He reached over and took a condom out of the pocket of his jeans, then tossed the pants back on the ground. "The next man wasn't rich and he wasn't all that smart, but he had something the other men lacked."

Paige gave him a sexy grin and touched his erection. "Let me guess. Was it something really, really big?"

He started to laugh, but then her hand tightened around him, and once again momentarily distracted him from his story. As she caressed him, he held on to what little was left of his self-control.

But after a minute or so, he reluctantly moved her hand away. "His love for her. That is what the other men lacked. The rich man coveted her because she was a rare beauty, and the wise man coveted her because she could bring him power. But the last man simply loved her because she was a wonderful person and being with her made him a better person."

"I like your story," she said, lying beneath him and urging him on top of her. "I like it very much."

"I thought you might," Max said, slipping between her thighs. For a second, he held her gaze, then he drove into her.

Paige gasped and smiled, tightening around him. "I like the story because he truly loved her."

Max slowly began to move. "Yes," he said. "He truly loved her."

Paige flashed him a wicked, sexy grin. "And he had a really, really big...heart."

He groaned. "That, too."

At her urging, he thrust into her again, setting a steady pace. He'd never felt closer to Paige, not just in body but also in spirit. However this case turned out, whatever happened when she learned who he was, he was determined to keep this woman in his life.

He held her gaze as she reached her peak. She was magnificent. Unbelievable. When she let out a cry of pleasure as she found her release, the joy in her voice pushed him over the edge.

And he knew he was exactly where he belonged.

PAIGE HELD MAX CLOSE. She couldn't remember ever being as happy as she was at the moment. In a strange, crazy way she owed her happiness to Brad. Because of that jerk, she'd run away to Key West.

All she needed to do was settle this thing with Brad and she could move forward. She could build a new life, a life she wanted to include Max. She couldn't pretend any longer—she was falling in love with him.

Max rolled off of her despite her protests. "I'm too heavy," he told her, then softened the loss with a kiss. "Not that I wouldn't like to stay there all night."

Paige cuddled against him. "I like the sound of that. We could make love all night long."

"Who's going to feed Sugar?"

The second he said the dog's name, Paige felt terrible. How could she forget her beloved dog?

Scrambling out of bed, she tossed Max's T-shirt to him. "The poor thing must be starving by now. I feel terrible about forgetting her."

"You've been busy," he pointed out, pulling on his boxers and jeans. "But you would have remembered."

Although Paige knew he was trying to make her feel better, she still felt like a louse. She got dressed as quickly as possible and then headed toward the door. Thankfully, Max was right on her heels.

"Sorry to rush us like this," she told him as they climbed in his car.

"That's okay. I figure we'll go to your place, take care of Sugar, and then maybe use your bedroom to take up where we left off."

"Definitely," she said as they pulled into the parking

lot of her apartment building. "I can hardly wait until—oh, my God."

The door to her apartment was wide-open. Max slammed on the brakes. "Dial nine one one."

Paige fumbled in her purse for her cell phone and did as he asked. As she explained what was happening, Max reached for his car door, but she shook her head.

"Wait for the police. They may still be inside," she said.

She heard barking and looked around. Sugar was in the doorway to the apartment. She was frantic, barking and yelping, and ran toward the stairs, then turned and ran the opposite direction away from the apartment.

"I've got to get her." Paige shoved the cell phone at Max, but then Max grabbed her arm.

"No. You can't go up there."

Paige started to argue, but then Max cursed and hit the gas, spinning them out of the parking lot.

"What are you doing?" she screamed. "I need to go get Sugar. She's scared."

"She'll be fine. Diane will take care of her. Right now, we've got bigger problems."

Paige looked behind her, hoping to see her dog and then froze.

Two men with guns were rushing down the stairs and heading their way.

11

PAIGE TRIED TO SPEAK, but Max pushed her head down. He drove out of the parking lot and down the street.

"Stay down, Paige. I have to lose them."

He took a sharp right, and she felt like the car was about to flip. "Max," she screamed.

"I know what I'm doing."

She looked over at him. He seemed so in control, so sure of himself. She had no idea if the men with guns were following them, but based on how often Max looked in his rearview mirror, they were.

"What about Sugar?" she said, knowing she should be worried about their lives, but unable to help herself.

"She's fine. She ran in the other direction. We'll get her after we take care of this scum." He spun the wheel to the left, and Paige screamed again.

"We're going to die," she said.

"No. We're not. Just hang on and trust me. You trust me, don't you, Paige?"

Paige was struggling to keep the hysteria growing inside of her under control. Max seemed so calm and cool but she was damn close to losing it.

"Do you trust me?" he repeated.

"Yes, yes," she said, holding on to the seat and trying to keep from falling on the floor.

He spun the wheel to the right, and she bit her lip to keep from screaming again.

He tossed her the phone. "I'm glad you trust me."

"Max, are we going to die?" She tried to raise her head and look behind them to see if the men were still following, but he gently kept her head down.

"Naw, we're not going to die. And keep down, Paige. It's safer that way."

For what felt like hours but was probably only minutes he drove them through the darkened streets of Key West. A couple of times, she heard a noise that sounded like a gunshot, but when she asked Max, he told her everything was under control.

"Paige, do me a favor and dial nine one one again," he said. "I think you hung up on them."

Although she still had her seat belt on, Paige was folded into a small lump. She moved her left hand and pulled out the phone.

"I'm not cut out for this," she said, then felt stupid for saying that. No one was cut out for this, although Max was handling it a lot better than she was.

"I know this is the worst possible time to say this, but I have to tell you how I feel. I think I love you," she said. She knew it was stupid, but she wanted him to know. "I wanted to tell you in case we don't survive."

He didn't say anything for a while, and she had no idea if it was because he was trying to keep them alive or because she'd stunned him silent.

Finally he said, "Yeah. Me, too. At least, I think."

As silly as it was considering everything that was happening to them, a rush of joy shot through Paige. He was feeling what she was feeling.

Max never took his gaze off the road, but she almost felt like he caressed her as he said, "I'm not going to let you die. Now dial nine one one and tell them to meet us in the parking lot of the old ShopSmart store."

He spun the car to the right again, making it almost impossible for Paige to dial. Her fingers kept slipping off the keys, but finally she managed to make the call.

As soon as the woman on the other end answered, Paige explained what was happening. Her heart was pounding and she was literally shaking. When the woman asked where they were, Paige admitted she hadn't a clue but repeated what Max had said about the parking lot.

"She said they're on the way."

He swerved the car to the left again. "Yeah, I can hear them."

After that everything happened so fast. They made one turn after another until Paige felt dizzy. She could hear the police sirens wailing, but it didn't seem to discourage the men chasing them.

Then suddenly, Max reached over and put his hand on her arm. "Hang on."

He slammed on the brakes. The car squealed to a stop. He kept Paige down as the police surrounded their car and the car following them.

Paige tried to figure out what was happening, but

Max kept her head down until the men in the car behind them had been pulled from their car and arrested.

Max opened his door and climbed out to speak to the police. Paige got out, too, and watched as the police put handcuffs on the two men. They were both yelling and screaming that they'd done nothing wrong, but when they saw her, they fell silent.

She started to take a step back, then stopped. She refused to be intimidated. They'd tried to kill her, but she was done being scared, done worrying if she or someone she loved was going to get killed.

She was done with all of this. She was tired of Brad. Whatever he wanted, she'd gladly give to him if she just knew what it was. There was no doubt this wasn't about jealousy. Brad had never loved her. No, this was about something else and she fully intended on finding out what that something was.

When one of the men started cursing at her, the officers moved them to squad cars and put them inside. Paige didn't care about them. She only cared about Max.

Glancing around, she saw that Max was talking to a man who was obviously in charge. Max stopped talking when he saw Paige and smiled at her. Paige felt her throat tighten at the sight of him. She was so glad he was okay, so glad he hadn't been hurt that she raced over and hugged him.

He felt solid and strong, and most importantly, alive. "I was so scared. Are you okay?" She leaned back to survey him closely. She didn't see any wounds but that didn't mean he wasn't hurt.

"I'm fine," he assured her, then kissed her soundly.

Paige clung to him, kissing him back with all the love she felt for him. She couldn't believe how close she'd come to losing him. If something had happened to Max, she wasn't sure she'd survive. Her heart would be permanently broken.

The sound of a man clearing his throat made Max end the kiss.

"I'm Detective Rogers," the man said, shaking Paige's free hand. "Glad you weren't hurt. You two were lucky those guys were dumb enough to keep chasing you even when they had to have seen the squad cars."

"I figured they would be so focused on us they wouldn't really notice what was happening around them," Max explained.

The detective nodded, then asked them to follow him to a police station down the street. As soon as they were in Max's car, Paige looked at him.

"About what I said earlier..."

Max glanced briefly at her. "I won't pretend not to know what you mean. Are you taking it back?"

"No. Actually, I wanted to tell you I no longer just think I love you. I'm sure I do."

She sat nervously waiting to hear what he'd say, but he didn't respond until they'd pulled in at the police station. Then he looked at her and said, "Yeah. Me, too."

Paige would have loved to kiss him, but the detective was already standing next to the car, so she climbed out. From that moment on, she didn't have a chance to talk to Max. The detective took them to a small room and asked them question after question for over an hour. The whole time, Paige kept feeling anxiety bubble up inside her.

Finally she asked, "Is there any way we could continue this back at my apartment? I'm worried about my dog."

The detective must have sensed her impatience because he said, "Let me check out his car first, then we'll go back to your apartment."

Relieved, Paige tried calling Diane as Max and the detective went to inspect the car. She tried several times but never got an answer. Finally she headed outside. The men were talking, but stopped as she approached.

"We'll drive you back to your apartment now," the detective said, leading the way to a police cruiser. Max and Paige got into the back seat while Detective Rogers and an officer got in the front.

"Run through your route for me again," the detective asked Max.

Max explained the streets he'd taken, carefully detailing what maneuvers he'd used to stay ahead of those guys.

Paige didn't like to think about it because more than once, Max stopped and he and the officers climbed out and searched certain areas. She knew they were looking for bullets. Those men had shot at them several times.

Right before they reached her apartment, Detective Rogers asked Paige, "You have no idea at all why Brad Collier is doing this?"

"No. I haven't a clue why he's after me," she said. When Max reached over and took her hand in his, she smiled at him. She loved this man so much, and tonight, he'd saved her life.

"I've called the police in Chicago. They've had no luck yet in getting in touch with Brad Collier and have no idea where he is. But they have talked with his father," Detective Rogers told her.

"The senator?" Max glanced at Paige. "Bet he didn't take the news well."

The detective nodded. "That's an understatement. The man is furious. He says you're making up this story."

They'd arrived at her apartment building. Paige pointed to the open door to her place. A couple of officers were stationed outside, but she could see beyond them to the mess inside. "Does that look like something I'm making up?"

Neither the detective nor Max answered her rhetorical question. There was no doubt whoever had ransacked her place was looking for something, something very important to them.

As they climbed out of the car, Max took the opportunity to hug her, holding her close and kissing the top of head.

"It's going to be okay," he murmured. "But you and I need to talk. I need to tell you something. Something about me that I should have told you a long time ago."

He sounded so serious that fear washed through Paige again. "Are you hurt after all? Did you find a wound?"

"No, it's nothing like that, although you may want to hurt me when you hear what I have to tell you."

Paige tried to follow what he was saying but it wasn't easy. There was so much noise and commotion around the apartment building that even this close she could barely hear him. "You're scaring me," she admitted. "What? What's wrong?"

"It's about why I'm here."

"Here in Key West or here with me?"

"Both," he said, his expression sad. "I need to explain a few things about my life."

Something was obviously bothering Max, and she wished they could be alone to talk about it. But they were surrounded by police officers and she needed to find Sugar.

"We'll talk after I find Sugar," she assured him. "I promise."

One of the officers standing in the doorway to her apartment told her, "Your neighbor has the dog."

The neighbor had to be Diane. Paige raced up the stairs and was almost to Diane's apartment when the door opened.

Sugar came bursting out, yapping and jumping all

over Paige. Paige felt herself crying but she didn't care. Sugar was okay. Max was okay.

Everything else would work out.

Diane came over and hugged her. "What in the world happened here? When I got home, your door was wide open, the police were all over the place, and Sugar was running around the parking lot."

Paige briefly explained about Brad and told her friend what had happened. When she mentioned how Max had saved them, she looked over her shoulder and found him standing at the end of the hall, smiling at her.

Paige gathered up Sugar and went to him. He hugged them both, her and her barking dog.

"Guess I was wrong about you, big guy," Diane said to Max. "Seems like you really care about Paige."

Once again, she felt him kiss the top of her head. "I love her," Max said simply.

Considering this was one of the worst nights of Paige's life, she should be hysterical, but she wasn't, and she knew that was because of Max. Just his presence helped her remain calm, but knowing he was feeling what she felt made her unbelievably happy.

"I know you have a lot to take care of tonight," Diane said. "So why don't you let Sugar stay with me for a few days until all of this gets sorted out?"

Although she hated being separated from Sugar, Paige admitted Diane's idea made sense. She couldn't leave the dog alone in her demolished apartment, and Sugar would be nervous in a new place.

Sugar needed to be somewhere familiar with some-one she knew. So after a few more hugs, Paige reluc-tantly let Diane take Sugar back to her apartment.

"You two take care of yourselves," Diane told Paige and Max.

After her friend went inside her apartment, Paige headed over to what was left of hers. She felt like cry-ing when she walked inside. Sure, her home hadn't been a palace, but it had been hers, and she'd liked it. The men had literally ripped it to pieces. All of her fur-niture was torn apart, all of her knickknacks thrown on the ground and smashed.

At that moment, she truly hated Brad. This had to stop. He was insane. What did he want? Why was he doing this?

"Mr. Walker," Detective Rogers said, coming in the door. "I forgot to give you your ID back." He handed Max his wallet.

Max took the wallet and tucked it into his back pocket. Then he looked at Paige. He looked defeated. "I need to talk to you."

Something was wrong. Very wrong. Paige took a step toward him. "What's wrong? Please tell me."

Before Max could say a word, Detective Rogers came over to stand next to her. "I know this seems terrible, but things could have been a lot worse. At least you weren't hurt. Mr. Walker's done fine taking care of you."

Paige nodded. "Yes. He saved my life."

"Yeah, well that's his job," the detective said.

At the detective's words, Paige froze. She couldn't have heard him right. "What did you say?"

Max groaned and headed toward her. "I have to explain something."

The detective picked up a broken vase and moved it aside. "Yes, you're lucky you had your own private investigator, or rather a security specialist, to take care of you. He knows a few things about protection." He glanced at Max. "You mostly do bodyguard work for corporations, right?"

Max was watching Paige. He didn't look at the detective as he answered, "Yeah." To Paige, he said, "Let me explain."

Paige felt cold. Ice cold, like she'd fallen into a deep frigid ocean and was rapidly sinking. This couldn't be happening. It just couldn't.

It took a couple of tries, but she finally managed to ask "A P.I.? You're a private investigator? Not a bartender, not some guy just out of the service?"

Her voice had an almost hysterical sound to it that she hated, but she couldn't help it. She'd *trusted* him. She'd completely *trusted* him.

This was a nightmare. There was no other way to view it. It was the worst nightmare she could imagine because she'd completely, absolutely believed in this man. It had hurt when Brad had disappointed her, but now, knowing that Max wasn't the man he'd pretended to be was far, far worse.

Paige wanted to cry. She wanted to scream. Instead she asked, "Who are you working for, or do I need to ask." She felt like the air was sucked out of her lungs. "You're working for Brad, aren't you?"

"No." He shook his head but she couldn't help wondering if he was lying about that, too. "Never. I would never work for someone like him."

She was going to be sick. Truly sick. This couldn't be happening. She couldn't have misjudged him. No one was that stupid.

"You need to let me explain," he said, moving toward her.

Paige was all too aware that Detective Rogers was watching them closely. He obviously found this very interesting. Why not? Wasn't it interesting to watch someone get her life torn apart? Wasn't that thrilling?

It must have been because the detective folded his arms across his chest, commenting, "I take it that Mr. Walker's background is a surprise to you." He frowned when he looked at Max. "Why didn't you tell her you worked for her father and had been hired to find her, and if necessary, to protect her?" He nodded toward Paige. "I'm sure she wouldn't have minded knowing her father cared about her."

Before Max could answer, Paige demanded, "You work for my *father*? My father probably told Brad everything I ever told you. My father never believed me when I said someone was after me. He just wanted me to come back home and continue with the engagement to Brad. Working for him is almost as bad as working for Brad."

"Your father wants you to come home," the detective said. "I spoke with him about a half hour ago and he's confirmed Mr. Walker's employment."

Paige didn't want to talk about her father right now. She wanted to find a bed to crawl into and pull the covers over her head.

Men. She hated them. All of them.

"Paige, I didn't tell your father a thing," Max insisted, and although Paige knew he was looking at her, she refused to make eye contact. "When I realized your father was telling Brad everything, I stopped updating him. I have no idea how they found you."

After a pause, during which she still didn't look at him, he asked, "You didn't call anyone, did you? You didn't tell anyone where you were, did you?"

It hit Paige like a ton of bricks. Her grandmother. She'd called her grandmother. But she'd used Max's cell phone, so they would have had no way to know about the call...unless they'd bugged her grandmother's phone.

Paige played back the conversation in her mind. She hadn't clearly come out and said where she was, but if Brad had been listening he might have been able to put the pieces together. Her grandmother had told her to go where it was sunny, and since Key West was also her grandmother's favorite place to visit, Brad probably had been able to figure it out.

She closed her eyes, and clenched her fists. When. When was this going to end? One little phone call had almost cost her her life.

"Paige," Max said softly. "I don't work for your father anymore. I haven't taken any money from him and I never will. Once I understood that he didn't believe what was happening and he was telling Brad what he knew, I stopped calling him. I stopped working for him several weeks ago."

"Then why are you still here?" She opened her eyes and pinned him with a direct gaze. "Why didn't you leave?"

Although she didn't add the words *before I fell in love with you*, they both knew that was what she really wanted to know.

"I stayed at first because I knew you needed protection," he said, his voice gravelly with stress. "Then I stayed because I not only wanted to protect you, but also because I fell in love with you."

Paige continued to stare at Max, her feelings a jumbled mess. She was so focused that it took her a few seconds to realize that Detective Rogers had asked her something.

"What?"

"You two are involved? Seriously involved?" he asked.

"Yes," Max said, his gaze never leaving Paige's face. He took a step toward her, but she in turn took a step back. "I only wanted to protect you, Paige. I thought if I told you the truth, you might run away. And if you did, Brad might have found you. I never meant to lie to you, but what would have happened if you'd come home tonight by yourself? Would you have known what to do? I've shown you a few self-defense moves, but not enough. I couldn't take the risk of you being unprotected. I couldn't risk you getting hurt."

This was too much for Paige to think about, too much to get her heart to accept all at once. He had a good point, but she couldn't think about it now. She glanced around her demolished apartment. Brad had destroyed her life. He'd ripped apart everything she held dear.

This had to stop.

But that paled in comparison to how she felt about Max right now. She glanced at him, realizing that she didn't know this man at all. She'd given him her love, her trust, and everything he'd told her had been a lie.

She didn't know what to think anymore, and her head hurt too much to think anyway.

There was only one thing of which she was certain— the time had come to get her life back. She was tired of lies, tired of running, tired of fear.

She'd been pushed around way too much and now it was time to end it, one way or another.

Still not looking at Max, she asked the detective, "Are we done here? I'm exhausted and would like to get some rest."

He nodded. "Sure. Where are you going since you can't stay here?"

"She can stay with me," Max said. "I have a motel room—"

But before he'd even finished speaking, Paige shook her head. "I'll find a place to stay."

"I have to know where you'll be in case I need to get

in touch with you," Detective Rogers explained. "There are a couple of nice hotels near the station. Want me to see if you can get a room at one of them?"

Paige nodded. Being near the police station would make it easier to sleep. She glanced at Max who looked horrible. For one split second, she felt sorry for him, and then she toughened herself. No. She wasn't going to feel badly for him. He'd brought this on himself.

"We still need to talk," he said.

"I need some time alone," she countered. And that was true. She needed time to get her head straight, time to finally deal with Brad. She couldn't deal with her crazy feelings for Max right now.

"I appreciate your help with the hotel," Paige told the detective.

While the man made the call, Paige avoided looking at Max. The tension in the room was almost over-whelming. She knew Max was upset, but what did he expect? That she'd say, "Gee thanks for lying to me and pretending you didn't know who I was while all this time you were working for my father."

He had to know he'd broken her heart.

"I was doing what I thought I needed to do to protect you, Paige," Max finally said softly, pain obvious in his voice. "But I need you to know, I never lied about my feelings for you."

She glanced at him. He looked as miserable as she felt. "I wish I could believe that."

"I got you a room," Detective Rogers said. "I'll have one of the officers drive you since I'm going to stay here a little longer and see what I can find," he said. "We still don't know why this man is after you, but considering the condition of this apartment, I'd say it isn't you he's after but rather something you have."

Shifting her attention away from Max to the other man, she said, "That's what I think, too, but I don't know what it could be. I don't have anything that belongs to him."

"That you know of," the detective pointed out. "But he obviously thinks you do, and it looks like he'll do about anything to get it back."

Paige rubbed her right temple. This whole thing made no sense. What did he want? She'd given him back all of his stuff when they'd broken up. She'd been very careful to return his things because she'd wanted him completely out of her life.

She had no idea what he wanted, and she wouldn't be able to figure it out tonight. She was tired, scared, and mostly, she felt like her heart had been used for soccer practice.

She wanted some peace and quiet, some time to think.

"Paige, don't leave like this," Max said again walking toward her. "I did what I had to do to keep you safe, and I'd do it again if I had to. I know you probably hate me right now, but that's okay. What matters is that you're safe."

Paige sighed. "We'll talk tomorrow," she said. That was the best she could do at the moment.

The detective arranged for an officer to take her to

the hotel. Paige would have liked to collect some of her things, but glancing around the apartment, she realized there was nothing left. Brad's goons had destroyed everything.

She felt like crying, but she wouldn't give into it. She wouldn't give into her feelings.

Now was the time to be strong.

She went with the officer, forcing herself to not look at Max as she left. Tonight, she'd decide what to do about all of the men in her life—Brad, her father, and most importantly, Max.

Then tomorrow, she'd take back control. These men would learn she wasn't the quiet mouse she'd been a few months ago. She was a woman in charge of her own life. No one was going to push her around again.

As soon as she got to her room, she took her first step toward freedom. When this mess had started, she'd called Brad a couple of times, thinking they could work things out. But he'd never taken her calls so she'd stopped trying.

But she was sure he'd take her call now. He was desperate and they both knew it, so she dialed Brad's cell phone, waiting impatiently for him to answer.

When he finally picked up, she said, "What is it that you want?"

"Wow, Alyssa, this is a surprise," Brad drawled, pretending innocence. "Did you miss me and long to hear my voice?"

"Drop the act. Meet me at the Sunset Café in Key West tomorrow at 6:00 p.m. You can tell me what you want and I'll give it to you. Then you get out of my life once and for all."

"Alyssa, I have no idea what you're talking about," he said, but this time she clearly detected laughter in his voice. The scum thought this was funny.

"Just be there," she said, hanging up on him.

She glanced around the room. The decor was typical hotel. Soothing colors, subtle patterns. Just what she needed to calm down and gather her thoughts.

She curled up on the bed, trying to think about Brad, but instead thinking about Max.

She'd thought he was her soul mate, the perfect man for her. A man she could love. A man she could trust.

She'd never expected him to lie to her.

For a long time, she let herself feel angry toward him. Then slowly, by tiny degrees, her innate fairness forced her to admit that he was right about one thing— if she'd known who he was, she would have run and kept running.

And Max was right about something else: she might have gotten herself killed. He'd definitely saved her life tonight. She had no doubt about that. Because of his quick thinking, they'd gotten away from those men tonight—men who'd obviously had no qualms about killing her to get what they wanted.

But Max had known what to do, and he'd risked his life to save hers.

That had been nice of him. Okay, more than nice. It had been brave of him. Plus, now that she was calm, she had to admit to herself that it wasn't like she hadn't lied to him, too.

Okay, so it turned out that he'd known all along who she was, but she hadn't known that when she'd been lying to him about who she was. She'd had a good reason for lying—her life depended on her being careful.

Just like he'd had a good reason for lying—her life depended on him not scaring her off.

She flopped onto her back and stared at the ceiling. She had to face facts—she missed Max. Her heart literally ached for him. No, she wished things hadn't happened the way they had, but on reflection, she could understand why he'd handled it that way.

With everything that had happened tonight, she supposed she could excuse herself for overreacting. But in the morning, when her emotions were settled, she would call Max and tell him she understood why he'd lied.

Feeling infinitely better, she gave into the exhaustion she'd felt for hours. Sleep claimed her quickly and deeply.

But she woke with a start when a hand slapped across her mouth and a man's voice whispered in her ear, "Hello, Alyssa. Long time no see."

12

PAIGE STRUGGLED against the hold Brad had on her, but his grip was too strong. For a few minutes, she fought, then stopped, forcing herself to be calm. Forcing herself to think.

"Give up?" Brad said, humor lacing his voice. "Figured you wouldn't last long."

That did it. Paige shifted slightly, then kicked, slamming her foot hard directly into his groin just like they'd practiced in the self-defense classes. Brad doubled over and howled in pain.

"You bitch," he spat.

When he let go of her, Paige used the opportunity to scurry to the opposite side of the bed. She started to scream, but before she got much sound out, Brad fumbled in his pocket and pulled out a gun.

"You scream and you'll get a one-way trip to meet your long deceased ancestors," he threatened. "Behave or be dead. The choice is yours. I don't really care."

Paige knew he meant it. He would kill her without blinking an eye. How had she been so wrong about this man? How had she ever believed in him?

"I won't scream," she said, glad her voice was relatively steady. The last thing she wanted was for him to know how frightened she was. When Max had shown the class those self-defense moves, he'd stressed how important it was to remain in control, to remain calm. She needed to think clearly if she was going to survive.

"I didn't expect to see you until tomorrow," she began, glancing around, then realizing the phone was over by him. That wouldn't work. Maybe she could make it to the sliding glass door leading to the patio. Carefully she started edging forward, but he shook his head.

"Stand still." He pointed the gun directly at her. "Or maybe I'll just kill you now."

Paige felt the air whoosh out her lungs. She should have seen this coming. She should have realized Brad wouldn't wait and meet her according to her terms. She knew now with utter certainty that he'd intended all along to kill her.

Fear tasted bitter in her mouth as she watched him walk across the room and grab her purse, his gun always pointed at her. She took a little pleasure in his noticeable wince as he walked. Good. She was glad she'd hurt him.

"You've been such a colossal pain in the ass to me for the last few months. I've had to chase you everywhere. It took up way too much of my time and way too much of my money."

He looked at her, obviously gloating at finally getting the upperhand. "But I figured it was only a matter of time before you called your grandmother. Bless her heart, that old guy who's always at her house didn't think a thing about letting a phone repairman in there a few weeks ago. They were clueless, even though my guys tried to break into that house when you were there."

He tore open her purse and turned it upside down. Everything inside dropped onto the foot of the bed. Brad groaned. "Still the packrat I see. Why do you carry all this junk with you?"

Paige didn't answer. Instead she scanned her mind, searching for anything Max might have taught her that she could use. Brad might be trying to appear calm, but he had a crazed look in his eyes. She knew it wouldn't take much to push him over the edge.

"What do you want? Tell me. You can have it, whatever it is, but I really don't think I have anything of yours," she insisted.

Brad studied her for a second, then with one hand, started rummaging through her stuff all the while keeping his attention—and the gun—trained on her. He didn't answer her. Instead he said, "I was so happy when you called your dear, sweet granny."

He smiled, and even though the lighting in the hotel room was dim, she could clearly see how much he was enjoying himself. He liked being in control this way. He liked having her completely under his power.

She'd always thought of Brad as handsome, with his styled dark blond hair and green eyes, but now she saw him for what he really was—a creep with way too much money and way too little honor.

He dug around in her things some more, then picked up the container of pepper spray.

"Afraid of me, Alyssa?" He laughed. "I guess you're not as soft and sweet as you used to be. Guess that new guy you're sleeping with has toughened you up."

Still smiling, he tossed the pepper spray down and continued to search. "God, Alyssa, what *don't* you have in this purse?" He held up her key chain and scowled at all the things hanging from it. "There wasn't this much stuff in your apartment, but I guess that's because everything you own is in your purse."

The second he glanced down at the contents of her purse again, she took a couple more steps toward the door. Her heart was beating so fast she thought she'd pass out. Fear was threatening to overwhelm her, but she kept telling herself to stay focused. That was the only way she'd survive.

When Brad looked back up, he didn't comment that she'd moved. Apparently he hadn't noticed.

"I bet you thought you were so smart," he said, a harsh edge to his voice. "Did you think you'd get away with it?"

"I have no idea what you're talking about," she said. "What is it that you want?"

He didn't answer her question. Instead he said, "Remember what it was like with us, Alyssa? We were pretty good together. But then you had to leave and ruin everything."

He had to be joking. They'd been terrible as a couple. Always fighting, always disagreeing. She'd thought he was charming when they'd first met, and although he'd had a few traits she hadn't liked, she'd still thought he was a decent man.

Then shortly after they'd gotten engaged, his behavior had changed. He'd become controlling, always asking what she was doing, where she was going. He'd been angry all the time, yelling at her constantly. Finally she couldn't take it any longer, so she'd called off the engagement.

He grabbed a handful of her belongings from the bed, stared at them, and then slung them across the room at her. She turned her head to keep them from hitting her face.

"So tell me, Alyssa, where's my disk? I'm losing my patience."

Baffled, she stared at him. His disk? "I don't know what you're talking about. I don't have a disk of yours."

"Do you think you can blackmail me with it? Is that your plan?" he said, his voice so soft she could barely hear him. "Do you hope you can embarrass my father? Get some money for yourself. You're a nasty piece of work."

This? From him? She took a deep breath and tried again. "Brad, I don't have a disk of yours." She kept her gaze focused on the gun in his hand. He wasn't holding it steady, which only heightened her fear.

"You know, I've been wondering about something. Does your new boyfriend find you as boring in bed as I did? I hear he's some sort of bodyguard type. Guess that means he's all muscles and limited brains. Sounds like the perfect guy for you, Alyssa."

She struggled to keep the panic inside her from fogging her brain. She needed to think clearly, needed to plan what to do. He kept up a steady stream of insults, but she ignored what he was saying.

There had to be something she could do, but she didn't want to get too close to that gun. "Brad, you've gone through my apartment and my purse. That's all I have."

He looked down at the stuff from her purse, and while he was preoccupied, Paige moved a couple more steps toward the door.

"And your car," he said nonchalantly. "My guys searched your car before they went inside your apartment."

"See? I don't have the disk you want. So leave me alone." She knew he wouldn't but she had to try.

Brad continued to dig through her stuff, and then stopped as if something had just occurred to him. "I guess once I'm done with you, I'd better go find muscle boy and take care of him, too. You've probably shared what was on that disk with him."

Max? He intended on killing Max, too. Paige felt her legs grow weak with terror, but she forced herself to stand firm. She wouldn't let him know how frightened she was.

"He doesn't have anything. I don't have anything," she tried to reason. "You've got nothing to gain by hurting us."

Brad kicked the bed. "This is getting more complicated than it needed to be, Alyssa. Blackmailing a senator's son is dangerous business," he said. "Who would have expected the perfect Alyssa Delacourte to stoop so low?"

"I'm not trying to blackmail you," she stated.

He ignored her. Instead he held her gaze and said, "By the way, if you take one more step toward the door, I will shoot you."

She could tell he was losing control. As each second ticked by, he got edgier, more frantic. Even though his voice was steady, his hands weren't. There was every chance he'd end up shooting her by mistake.

"I don't have your disk," she said quietly, trying to soothe him. "Even if I did, I would never blackmail you, Brad."

"But I know that's what you planned on doing," he said. "You want to get me. I know you do. You were always doing things I told you not to do." He looked at his watch. "I'm tired of this game, Alyssa. Where is the disk?"

Paige suddenly decided to shift her tactic. "You know, Brad, I'm surprised to find out you're not the wonderful businessman the whole world thinks you are," she said, trying to goad him into making a mistake. "Your father's connections brought you a lot of clients and turned you into the most successful financial advisor in Chicago. So what's on the disk? Evidence that you did some creative money management and helped yourself to some of those impressive assets of your clients?"

She could tell from his expression that was exactly what was on the disk. He leaned toward her and warned, "Be very careful what you say. Like I told you, I long ago lost my patience with you. Give me the disk and I'll let you go."

She knew he wouldn't. She was positive that the second Brad thought he knew where this disk was, he'd kill her. She had to think. There had to be something she could do.

A tiny flicker of movement outside on the patio caught her eye. She knew immediately it had to be Max. Like Brad, he must have followed her.

But rather than being relieved, her fear only increased. Brad definitely would kill Max without giving it a second thought.

"Let me rephrase that," he said when she didn't immediately answer. "Tell me where the disk is or I'll shoot you right now."

She knew he wouldn't shoot her, not until he'd gotten the disk. But Brad would shoot Max, and there was no way to come in from the patio and not be seen. Brad would have plenty of opportunity to kill Max.

Paige racked her brain for a way out of this, some way to get Max safely inside.

Finally she looked directly at Brad until he made eye contact with her, then she said, "You'll never get away with this. The police know all about you."

"But they don't know about the disk," he pointed out.

"But they do know you're after me and they also know I'm staying at this hotel. They told me they'd have someone watch my room tonight. I'm sure they're well aware that you are here," she lied, hoping he'd believe her.

Doubt crossed his face. He wasn't sure whether she was telling the truth or not. Good. She needed that doubt. She needed him to look away from Max.

Knowing that Brad was watching her closely, she deliberately glanced at the connecting door to her room. It was just a split-second glance intended to look casual. It worked. Brad spun and immediately headed toward the door.

"They're in the next room, aren't they?" He opened the door on her side. The door to the room next to hers was still closed, but she could tell Brad was convinced someone was on the other side.

It didn't matter that no one was there because while Brad was focused on the connecting door, she moved silently and unlocked the sliding glass door.

She'd never been so happy to see someone, but at the same moment, she was terrified that something would happen to him. She loved him so much.

She needed to help. Scanning the stuff Brad had tossed at her, she spotted her key chain and picked it up. Maybe this thing would bring her some luck after all.

Brad was still looking at the connecting door. He

must have had second thoughts about opening the other door because he started to back away. That was the last thing Paige wanted him to do since then he'd notice Max on the patio.

"Why don't you find out if someone is really there?" Paige said loudly, trying to cover up the whisper the sliding glass door made when Max opened it. "Are you afraid, Brad? I thought you weren't afraid of anything."

Brad looked over his shoulder at her. "I wasn't sure before, but now I'm convinced someone is there. That would make you really happy, wouldn't it, Alyssa? I'd get killed and you could sell the disk to the press."

"You're disgusting," she screamed, adding on more and more insults to cover up the noise of Max entering the room. "I hate you," she finally said, tacking on the last part deliberately because she knew it would surprise Brad, and it did. Despite everything he'd done to her, he seemed genuinely surprised she hated him.

He stood still for a moment staring at Paige. Then, even though Max had hardly made any noise, Brad spun toward him and pointed the gun.

Paige screamed and didn't even hesitate. She flew across the room, tackling Brad and crashing to the ground. When he started to shove her away, she hit him hard across the face with her key chain. Brad screeched, and while he was trying to recover, Paige next slammed her hand into his nose, then kicked him in the groin again. He howled in pain.

Paige stood up and glared down at him. "You bastard," she said, still poised for more trouble.

Max walked over to stand next to her. He looked down at Brad, then leaned over and picked up the gun.

"I'll call the police," he said, walking around her to the phone. He pointed the gun at Brad. "I have your gun."

Brad must have known better than to mess with either of them. He stayed where he was, occasionally whimpering, but other than that, he was silent. Paige kept looking at Max. He was all business, his attention entirely on Brad. She supposed that was the smart thing to do. Until he was in police custody, they had to play this safe.

Since the hotel was near the police station, it didn't take long for several officers to be at the door. Paige walked over and let them in. She wasn't surprised to see Detective Rogers with them.

"I had a feeling something else might happen tonight," he said when he saw Paige. When he noticed Brad crumpled on the floor, he turned to Max. "I see you took care of this."

Max shook his head. "Never laid a finger on him. Paige did it all on her own."

She didn't miss the touch of pride in his voice. She looked at him and found him watching her closely. She could clearly read what he was feeling on his face. Admiration. Respect.

Love.

Without hesitation, she smiled at him. "I had a good teacher."

Detective Rogers looked from one to the other. "I see things have worked out between the two of you."

Max slowly returned Paige's smile, but she could see uncertainty mingling with hope in his gaze. "I'm not sure."

She headed across the room toward him, swerving to bypass Brad, who was cursing as the officers cuffed him and read him his rights.

"You should be sure," she said, touching the side of his face. Then she leaned up and kissed him. Max gathered her close, holding on to her like he'd never let her go.

One kiss followed another, until once again, the sound of someone clearing his throat made them pull apart.

"Sorry to do this to you a second time." Detective Rogers had a big smile on his face. "But I need to ask you some questions."

Max had his arms around Paige, and she'd never been happier in her life. Nothing could bother her when she was with the man she loved. Not the insults Brad hurled at her as the police escorted him from the hotel room, and not the endless stream of questions she and Max had to endure over the next few hours.

When they were finally done, Detective Rogers shook their hands and told them he'd be in touch. Then they walked outside, into the morning sunlight where an officer was waiting to drive them back to her apartment.

Paige would have liked to talk to Max on the drive over, but since they weren't alone, she decided to wait. When they reached her apartment building, she headed toward the stairs, then stopped.

"The utility closet." She grinned at Max and sprinted to the back of the building. When they reached the small room, she unblocked the door and walked inside. "I put a couple of boxes in here when I first moved in."

As she routed through the boxes looking for hers, she could feel Max watching her. She knew he was nervous. She was nervous, too.

"Eureka." She pulled out one of the boxes and opened it. There were books, photos, and a whole stack of disks.

"If I had to guess, I'd bet one of these is the one Brad wants."

"We'll take them to Detective Rogers," Max said.

He was walking toward the door when she said, "I understand why you lied."

Max turned to look at her. "Do you?"

"Yes. You wanted to protect me. Just like you did tonight. You followed me to the hotel, didn't you?"

He nodded. "I couldn't stand it if anything ever happened to you." His voice was gruff with emotion as he added, "I love you. You mean everything to me."

She smiled at him, joy rushing through her. "I love you, too. And I realize this was what you meant by trust. Although we weren't always honest with each other, we could always trust one another."

"You'll always be able to trust me," he said. Then, he added, "That is, if you're interested in a future together."

He was so sweet. So kind. No wonder she loved him so much.

She walked over to him and wrapped her arms around his neck. "Are you asking me to spend my life with you? Because it sure sounded that way to me."

"That's because that was exactly what I was asking." He noticeably hesitated, then added, "If you're interested."

She pretended to think. "Sharing our future. Hmmm. You know, that sounds awfully like a proposal to me."

Max gently lifted her arms away from his neck, and then dropped to one knee. Paige tried to tell him it wasn't necessary, but he wouldn't listen to her.

"We didn't do anything in our relationship the traditional way, but I'm doing this right." He held her hand, gazed into her eyes, and asked, "Will you marry me?"

Paige could feel tears streaming down her face, but she didn't care. All she cared about was the incredible man before her.

"I would love to marry you," she said, leaning down and tugging him to his feet. "I'm the luckiest woman alive."

"I guess tossing that spilt salt over your shoulder did the trick," he said with a grin.

"Maybe." She brushed his lips with her own, lingering when he kissed her back. Then she broke off the kiss and said, "Personally, I think my luck changed when I met and fell in love with the most fantastic person in the whole world. You'll love me forever, right?"

"I swear on my brother's head," he said with a laugh as he slid his arms around her. "And you can't do better than that."

Epilogue

"THINK WE HAVE ANY chance of making it out of here alive?" Max surveyed the room, his hopes fading fast. Danger was everywhere.

Next to him, Paige sighed. "I don't know. It could be tricky. Ever been in a situation this tough before?"

Max counted the people between them and the door. Tim was waiting and so was Emilio. In fact, all of the wedding guests had formed two lines, leaving a narrow walkway to the front door. Even Paige's father and grandmother were part of the gang.

Every single person lined up looked suspicious. But the clincher was his brother, who stood near the front, a broad grin on his face, a devious glint in his eyes.

"I've survived a lot, but this..." Max gathered Paige close and dropped a kiss on her lips. "This doesn't look good."

"Come on, you two. If you want to leave on your honeymoon, you're going to have to go by us," Tim said in a sing-song voice. "But don't worry. We won't do anything to you."

Any chance he had of being believed disappeared when the crowd broke into laughter. Oh, yeah. These people were planning something.

"Tim, you're a terrible liar," Paige hollered, wrapping her arms around Max. "You promised you wouldn't do anything to us if we had the wedding reception here."

Tim's eyes grew wide and he feigned innocence. "Did I? I must have forgotten."

Max made a growling noise. For eight months, he and Paige had planned this wedding. Everything had been perfect. The ceremony had gone off without a hitch. The reception had been great. For a while, he'd even started to think Paige had been right to hold the wedding in Key West rather than in Chicago.

But now...he surveyed the gauntlet between them and the door. This had been a big mistake.

"Come on, it won't be so bad," Travis teased. "You can take it. You're tough."

"Remind me to kick you out as my partner when we get back to Chicago," Max told his brother.

Travis laughed. "Coward."

That was it. Max gave Paige another lingering kiss, then told her, "Every day, my love for you grows. I love you more than life, so I'll protect you. I can shield you with my body."

"I love you, too," Paige said. "And I'm not worried about these people. We can take them. These last few months have been magical, and I'm looking forward to our long and happy life together."

Max was thrilled to hear her say that. Nodding at the lines that had formed beside Tim and Travis, he said, "Assuming we make it through that."

Paige hugged him again, then picked up her purse.

With a wink, she shifted a little. "Block me from their view."

It sounded like a good idea. "Yeah, I'll block you so whatever they plan on throwing at us doesn't—"

"We're not going down without a fight." Paige shoved something into his hands. "Ready?"

Max glanced down. Whipped cream. She'd given him a can of whipped cream? He raised one eyebrow. "Ready for what?"

"Rumour has it they plan on getting us with chocolate body paint as we run by. I figured turnabout would be fair play, so I grabbed these two cans from the kitchen a couple of minutes ago. We'll give them a taste of their own medicine."

Her smile was sexy and bright, and Max had never loved her more than he did at this moment. Life with Paige was going to be amazing."

"Come on, Max," Travis said baiting him. "Show your new bride how brave you are."

Paige smiled. "So, Max, are you with me?"

He looked at the can of whipped cream in his hand, and then at the woman he loved so deeply. "Yeah, I'm with you. I'll always be with you—every step you take."

They began to run.

HARLEQUIN®

Temptation®

When the spirits are willing...
Anything can happen!

Welcome to the Inn at Maiden Falls, Colorado. Once a brothel in the 1800s, the inn is now a successful honeymoon resort. Only, little does anybody guess that all that marital bliss comes with a little supernatural persuasion....

Don't miss this fantastic new miniseries. Watch for:

#977 SWEET TALKIN' GUY by Colleen Collins
June 2004

#981 CAN'T BUY ME LOVE by Heather MacAllister
July 2004

#985 IT'S IN HIS KISS by Julie Kistler
August 2004

THE SPIRITS ARE WILLING

Available wherever Harlequin books are sold.

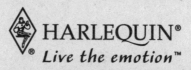

HARLEQUIN®
Live the emotion™

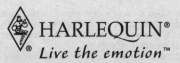

If you enjoyed what you just read,
then we've got an offer you can't resist!

Take 2 bestselling love stories FREE!

Plus get a FREE surprise gift!

Clip this page and mail it to Harlequin Reader Service®

IN U.S.A.
3010 Walden Ave.
P.O. Box 1867
Buffalo, N.Y. 14240-1867

IN CANADA
P.O. Box 609
Fort Erie, Ontario
L2A 5X3

YES! Please send me 2 free Harlequin Temptation® novels and my free surprise gift. After receiving them, if I don't wish to receive anymore, I can return the shipping statement marked cancel. If I don't cancel, I will receive 4 brand-new novels each month, before they're available in stores. In the U.S.A., bill me at the bargain price of $3.80 plus 25¢ shipping and handling per book and applicable sales tax, if any*. In Canada, bill me at the bargain price of $4.47 plus 25¢ shipping and handling per book and applicable taxes**. That's the complete price and a savings of 10% off the cover prices—what a great deal! I understand that accepting the 2 free books and gift places me under no obligation ever to buy any books. I can always return a shipment and cancel at any time. Even if I never buy another book from Harlequin, the 2 free books and gift are mine to keep forever.

142 HDN DZ7U
342 HDN DZ7V

Name	(PLEASE PRINT)	
Address	Apt.#	
City	State/Prov.	Zip/Postal Code

 * Terms and prices subject to change without notice. Sales tax applicable in N.Y.
** Canadian residents will be charged applicable provincial taxes and GST.
   All orders subject to approval. Offer limited to one per household and not valid to
   current Harlequin Temptation® subscribers.
   ® are registered trademarks owned and used by the trademark owner and or its licensee.

TEMP04   ©2004 Harlequin Enterprises Limited